CW00850437

THE CONFLUENCE

Telwyn

authorHOUSE®

AuthorHouse™ UK Ltd.
500 Avebury Boulevard
Central Milton Keynes, MK9 2BE
www.authorhouse.co.uk
Phone: 08001974150

First published by AuthorHouse 2/20/2010

ISBN: 978-1-4490-7125-7 (sc)

This book is printed on acid-free paper.

Drawn by Sophia Mazzotta
2008

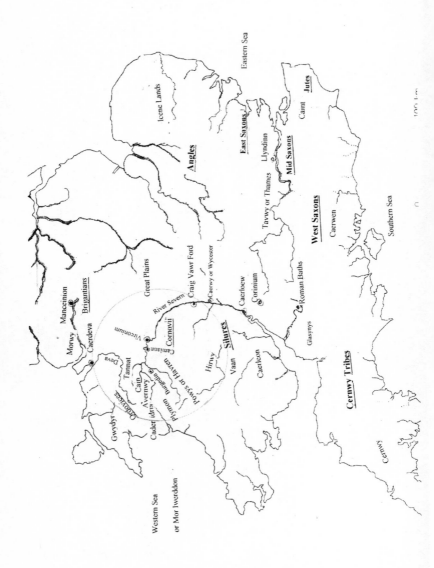

Addenda

<u>Various Celtic tribes</u> – Cornovii, Ordivices, Silures, Brigantians.

<u>Rivers</u>' – Deva, Severn and tributaries Avernwy, Tannat, Cain etc.

<u>Forts & Settlements</u> – Burgedin, Camlann, Caerdeva, Virconium, etc.

<u>Mountains</u> - Cader Idris, Cader Berrwyn, Gwydyr etc.

Locations in the book are authentic and also 6th century Celtic saints of Welsh history; however some of their spellings are deliberately altered to preserve their pronunciation in the English languge. Also some place names are slightly changed such as Talwrn for Trallwng (Welshpool), and as to emphasize the long Welsh vowels; Berwyn is spelt Berrwynn, Taran-Tarran, Bran-Braan, etc.

Welsh equivalence of 'v' is the single letter 'f', and Dyfa is pronounced Deva, also two 'dd's' is '<u>the</u>', and thus Blaidd (Wolf) is pronounced 'Blithe'.

Because the Welsh language is highly infiltrated with Latin words its original names' for Earth, Sun and Moon are long lost. Therefore I have substiuted with equvillance in purer Scottish Gaelic, - Talam, Grian and Gelach respectively.

~

CHAPTER I

ARRIVES IN CYNWEDYN

Berrwynn falls in battle and encounters a mysterious physician. He arrives in a mystifying world and meets Androssan the Ageless, and the enchanting Bronwen. Berrwynn agrees to relate his life story.

"Berrwynn of Burgedin is dead and all is lost", these were the first words the wounded warrior heard on regaining consciousness. And in hearing; and as yet incorrect declaration, Berrwynn assumed he was at the brink of a warrior's ultimate liability in war.

In having sustained a mighty blow to his head Berrwynn was fortunate that Tarran's sturdy Roman helmet saved his immediate life. However the sword's downward glance had cut through his leather shoulder guard causing a severely bleeding gash.

When the burly Angle warrior; who delivered the blow, was about sever the wounded leader's head and gain his reward, he was himself speared in the back and fell across and shielded Berrwynn, and inadvertently saved his life.

Lying beneath the dead warrior's heavy weight and in extreme pain; Berrwynn drifted in and out of consciousness, cognisant he vividly recollected his past life and primarily of Tresoara his long lost first love. He also beheld visions of his mother Rhiannon; and who had lavished her love and protection on him and his sister Aurian after the tragic death of their father. And shamefully recollected how his mother toiled and schemed to retain his rightful inherited leadership, and of choosing Marchell as his prospective wife, and which he all vainly forsook.

He pictured the shimmering waters of Llyn Tegid and where he as child and young man enjoyed exquisite summers with Carrog tribe cousins, and his eyes welled with tears when recalled the last time he spent there with his love Tresoara.

Under the hefty dead warrior's pressing weight Berrwynn desperately fought for his breath, and deliriously envisaging was drowning in the mud he cried out and fortunately his voice alerted some surviving comrades.

They were relieved he was still alive and rescuing him from under the corpse they gathered around his scarcely recognisable blood covered body, but in observing his wounds' they held very little hope of his recovery.

Immeasurable time later Berrwynn visualised a tall figure bending over him examining his wounds, and thereafter his head was raised and was given a much needed drink of water. However he then again lost unconsciousness and brought to reality by a nauseous substance in his nostrils, he then felt balm gently applied to his painful body. The stranger in seeing Berrwynn had regained consciousness soothingly assured him it would assist heal his wounds, and now feeling a little more relaxed; and this time it was gentle sleep which overtook his weary body.

Later; and slightly more aware Berrwynn hazily focused the stranger vigorously pounding a mortar; and suddenly its contents' was unceremoniously poured down his unwilling throat. However the bitter tasting mixture caused him to severely retch and the stranger; whilst muttering some uncomplimentary phrases he took a leather bottle from a pouch and poured yellowish liquid into the bowl. This time he upheld Berrwynn's head and allowed him to gently sip, and when tasted found pleasant and recognised was 'medd' or honey wine, and soothed his dry throat.

Previous retching had reactivated the pains his head and wounded shoulder and he again writhed in agony, and seeing his profound discomfort again the stranger incoherently muttered an sounding as "Damn, this is the very last of my medical containments" and from an elaborate casing produced an alchemist's phial. Berrwynn then felt similar to a bee sting in his buttock, and he immediately entered a blissful sleep.

He dreamed that he was passing through a gossamer veil similar to a cascading waterfall and then drifting backwards down a dark sloping cave and lit by lights intermediately flashing from hidden cavities. Where illuminated ghostly presence of people alongside and whom Berrwynn recognised as of long dead friends and warriors he had known. The near skeletal figures uttered no words but held out their arms as if to embrace him, and instinctively he avoided their touch.

Eventually from over his shoulder emerged a gleam of day light from end of the cave and subsequently he landed onto something comfortably soft, and helplessly lay there feeling warm breezes soothing his wounded body.

An unknown time later he glanced to his side and discovered he was amidst a most colourful countryside of lush meadows full of flowers, and birds in the surrounding trees sang sweeter than he had ever heard before. And judging by the absolutely colourful surroundings began wondering whether a dream or was now dead and in Nevol; the celestial paradise of his Celtic beliefs.

But a little time later when attempted to turn away from the sun's glare marring his eyesight he discovered that his body was still very weak and his right shoulder was again painful. Berrwynn was now even more puzzled, and concluded that he must still be alive as religiously knew that in Nevol there was no pain or sorrow, and pursuance of explanations wearied him and supposedly he again slept.

After intermittent bouts of unawareness the mistiness of his mind slowly began to clear and he again began wondering where was, and how long lain helpless, and suddenly he recalled the sombre words he heard spoken on the battlefield. 'Berrwynn is dead, and the war is lost', and stark horrors of his experiences on the bloody battle flooded his mind and was overwhelmed with grief at probable deaths of his friends and comrades.

Thereafter thought of his family's fate and finally of his own future if survived his wounds and then another and most horrifying thought jolted his mind. 'Was he now maybe a prisoner of the enemy? , and he dared not contemplate the torture which may now befall him'.

Recovering a little more became aware that he was comfortably wrapped in a clean fleece laid on straw bed and above him a reed roof and perceived it was the interior of an open sided rude shack. These simple but ample comforts greatly alleviated his anxieties of being a captive; as such amicable consideration would never be afforded an enemy prisoner.

Again drifted into a relaxed sleep and an unknown time later he was awakened by sounds of jubilant young voices and a group of four young children came into view carrying fishes on a hooked stick. The children were visibly startled at the sight of the wounded warrior, and whilst two nervously stayed a short distance away the others rushed into the woods, and returned with armed men.

Much to Berrwynn's relief the warriors spoke the language of ancient pre-Celtic mountainous tribes the Romans called Ordivces, and a tongue he was familiar as was spoken by his mother; a native of Ordivces' Carrog tribe.

When he answered them in their own dialect they immediately became friendlier and he was invaded with questions, "Who was he"? and the inevitable question he could not at present answer, "How come he to their domain"?

In trying to explain Berrwynn spoke of the great battle; and curiously they had no knowledge, and incredibly when he then mentioned the Angles, Saxons and later the Romans it also confused them, and replied they knew of no such tribes.

However, when conferred the part a mysteriously tall figure had played in his recovery they immediately proclaimed he was none other than Androssan; their spiritual guide and physician.

The priest's name of Androssan greatly puzzled Berrwynn as was meaningless in all three local languages he was conversant, and also his presence contradicted Roman's claim that they had eliminated the druids many years earlier.

He also found it strange their speech excluded familiar Celtic and also all Latin words introduced since Roman conquest, and he contemplated was most probably due to their complete isolation.

Berrwynn was also in dire need of answers, and proceeded to question by asking "What tribe am I amongst"? and they replied "We have always dwelled here, and we are called the Maengwyn people as we revere the glistening white rocks".

Berrwynn requested meeting Androssan to thank him for his salvation; and when saw he noticed the supposed druid was a physically distinguishing figure with white hair and long beard. Taller than the average Briton, and Berrwynn nurtured feelings had previously known, however acknowledged was probably mistaken as to his resemblance to warriors he had known. The descendants of a race of people from cold northern lands and who long ago were wrecked on Albany's rocky coast; and unable to return stayed and intermarried with native Celtic peoples.

Androssan was dressed in a long brown garb and tied in around his middle by a matted straw rope and draped around his shoulders was a goat skin cape, hiding a leather pouch where kept his belongings. His most peculiar attire however were his footwear, strangely long and containing metal parts and assumedly were dilapidated cut down knee length boots the Romans wore in Britain's winters.

Berrwynn was sympathetically informed the great battle had been lost and with great loss of life, and he Androssan was commissioned by the gods to bring him to this sanctuary in the mountain wilderness as to recover from his wounds.

Further informed, that when Berrwynn clung to life he was made comfortable as was possible, and fortunately able to feed with devised liquid diet, and physically strong managed to survive the ordeal.

Androssan however modestly claimed his recovery was mainly due to a band of dedicated women who secretly nursed him throughout incapacity, and learning of their kindness Berrwynn requested be called so he could personally thank them. He found the women were also modest recipients of their caring deeds, amongst them was an outstandingly attractive maiden with long jet-lack hair and wonderfully soft white skin.

When Berrwynn saw her face his heart leaped and instinctually he cried out "Tresoara, you have come back to me". However his spontaneous outburst only caused the maid to profusely blush; and he noticed the bloom it brought to her face further enhanced her youthful beauty. But to his utter disappointment, she and highly embarrassed replied. "Sir you are mistaken, my name is Bronwen", and as not for others pressing forward preventing she would surely gone and hid.

Berrwynn could not believe was possible for two persons to be so physically alike, but resemblance to his dear dead wife perturbed him and again harboured thoughts whether continuance of a dream. But whether dream or not; and in spite of his utmost loyalty to his dearest Tresoara he felt an immense sense of relief, and also much delight as to the maid's presence.

A while later Androssan approached and declared. "This is Bronwen, wife of Peredin the leader of Maengwyn people" and then added "This is the maiden on learning of your plight persuaded a band of dedicated women to secretly attend to your needs".

After their now formal introduction Berrwynn gently took Bronwen's hand and kissed it, and she again glowingly blushed whilst shyly backed away and quickly disappeared in amongst the crowd.

When Androssan first introduced Bronwen he noticed had referred to her as Peredin's wife but later contradicted referred to her as 'maiden' and wondered whether he was confining something, or was merely a slip of the tongue.

The more he became acquainted with Bronwen the more she seemed to resemble Tresoara, and not only physically she was also demure and gradually became less bashful of his attention, and they enjoyed interesting conversations.

Berrwynn also much enjoyed the tribe's people friendly company and was continually surrounded by curious children asking all sorts of questions of life outside their confined valleys. Realising that most tribal members were ignorant of life beyond their immediate surroundings and knew absolutely nothing of history; he asked Androssan as whether he allow him to teach them.

Androsan however was curiously hesitant and it amazed Berrwynn that he preferred they wallow in ignorance, but later learnt the strange reasons of his hesitancy.

Recalling Androssan previously announcing he had been commissioned by the gods to bring him to the sanctuary; but then unwell, he accepted his vague assertions. And now his health improved; Berwynn had the curiosity and will to question his unconvincing claim he was in league with usually un-communicative gods.

Androssan agreed to offer a preliminary explanation, and firstly revealed that he was not a druid but a alchemist, and far more bewilderingly he announced that he was not of the present, or of the past, but of far-far into the future.

Berrwynn was again astounded, and on his further questioning Androssan explained it was all the gods permitted him to reveal at the present time. Unsatisfied and thoroughly disappointed Berrwynn ceased further questioning as he was concerned the more avid exclamations might again deteriorate his health.

Though enjoyed Maengwyn people's friendly support Berrwynn state of mind needed very little cause to recede into uncontrollable depressions, and began to suffer from nightmares. Unceasingly he tortured himself of guilt that his past leadership's inadequacy had caused deaths' of his comrades and of his faithful followers.

The knowledge Androssan's medicines were exhausted worsened his condition and as no one could now aid him and despairingly wandered into the woods. Alone with his thoughts it suddenly occurred to him the possibility of some druidic cures and with renewed hope Berrwynn returned to the settlement. However, when enquiring of a druidic priest physician or wizard or such, he was informed they had Androssan; and that his wisdom was superior to all others.

Berrwynn castigated himself in forgetting of Androssan's claim of a futuristic alchemy knowledge, and if true, it was therefore possible that he was also capable of concocting suitable druidic like medicines.

Seeking his advice, Androssan explained that though an alchemist he had no physicist's dispensary experience, but he relished the challenge confirming he would use futuristic alchemy knowledge to produce their equivalence.

Thereafter he returned to his laboratory to restudy of his old medical researching manuals to find minerals and plants and of which their essence equalized constituents of his known futuristic or modern medicines.

Within weeks Androssan returned with dispensed formulae, however he warned that some of its constituents were extremely hallucinogenic, and as untested on humans he did not wholly know had side effects.

He then; and most alarmingly, revealed that if were over subscribed a patient could possibly enter into a state of an extraordinary and colourful existence, and of which he had not as yet an antidote.

Hearing this Berrwynn became apprehensive and questioned its components, but Androssan however was proud of his achievement, and he was only too happy oblige. Revealing had first drawn water from the mineral 'Glowing Spring'; and so called as glowed in moonlight, then added a preparation of various plants to make a compound. However, he revealed not the baneful yew, mistletoe and deadly solenium berries ingredients, as Berrwynn's knowledge of their deadly poisons would cause him refuse the medicine.

A mere mortal of Berrwynn's time would not understand that when scientifically synthesized in his laboratory these ingredients were made harmless and ingestible. Androssan in needing very minute quantity the surplus compound was preserved for his scientific experiments, also possible future medicinal uses.

Though druidic fungi was controversially highly hallucinogenic, it was liberally included, and the finished medicine was poured into a bowl and honey added to sweeten. Finishing his performance presentation Androssan declared that his wonder cure was to be taken before retiring at nigh and with several generous goblets of his potent yellow wine.

It was not long before Berrwynn felt physically and possibly psychologically cured and he no longer agonisingly dwelt on his past's horrifying experiences or also suffered the recurring nightmares, and soundly slept well into the day.

Having successfully counteracted his demons Berrwynn felt extraordinarily invigorated, and he again inquisitively questioned Androssan's revelations concerning his mysterious dream of his passage to this place.

Androssan indignantly confirmed what had revealed was not of a dream but his regressive journey through centuries of earth time, and looking at Berrwynn's face he saw that he distinctively doubted what he revealed.

The master then hesitated and took the opportunity to refill his goblet, and then slowly continued and proclaimed. "This place you have entered is of another time dimension, but its explanation is far beyond a mere mortal's presumption, however is best described as 'Cyn-wedyn', meaning 'Pre-after'".

Throughout his young life Berrwynn enjoyed listening to the bards extolling extraordinary tales, and of which only the few gullible accepted as was common knowledge that bards often concocted stories as to entertain for money. Similarly he enjoyed Androssan's narrations, but remained equally dismissive of his claimed phenomenal connections and occurrences.

Native Maengwyn people were immensely interested in the much travelled warrior, and this gave Androssan an inspiration for an experimental therapeutic remedy that he had read; and in what referred as his modern day medical journal.

He suggested that every evening after they had eaten; and instead of the usual bards songs, poetry and storytelling around the fire; that Berrwynn entertain the tribe's people by telling them his life story.

At first Berrwynn was apprehensive of casting his mind back to horrors he had seen and suffered as feared it might re-activate his depressive illness, Androssan however assured. "According to my medical journal, facing one's fears has opposite effects".

After much thought Berrwynn decided to accept the physiological experiment, but jovially aired was on one condition, that it excluded his romantic encounters and of which had to remain a secret between him and his lady friends.

In preparation of his epic story Berrwynn retrieved to a glade in the woods, and through two phases of the moon god Gelach he thought back and recorded on a cloth with scorched stick the main points of his short but extraordinary life.

When eventually returned announcing he was ready to address the tribes' people, he was amazed so many people had gathered to hear his story. Not only local tribe's people but also others and from far distant valleys sat eagerly awaiting to hear his amazing warrior's story.

CHAPTER II

INTRODUCTION

Peoples of exiled Celtic Powyse/Coronvii Burgedin faction. Cadwaladr's death. Leadership' conflicts. Gethinn the tyrant. Exile. Rhiannon and Antonius. Gethinn assassinate. They Return to Burgedin. Berrwynn meets Tarran and then returns.

More than five hundred years had past since beginning of Roman conquest of Britain and over a hundred years since withdrawn their legions to defend Rome from barbarian invaders.

Remaining Romans thereafter intermarried with native Celts or descendants of many nationalities of which the legions had consisted, and thereon only the very few hierarchies could honestly claim to be of pure Roman blood.

Known to Romans as Cornovii, this Powyse tribe previous to their conquest had occupied lands bordering the central western mountainous region, and conquest caused many to seek refuge in adjoining woody hill valleys. Living amongst the indigenous inhabitants; and whom Romans regarded primitive and called them Ordovices – and meaning 'The Stone Hammerers'.

A very long time earlier the Ordovices had also been dispersed by then invading Celts and similarly they had also sought safety in the inhospitable northern and western mountainous' regions.

The now exiled Celts lived in small splintered groups various small woody valleys. The Burgedin faction claimed that they were the true Powyse or Cornovii' inheritors, as they had retained descendants of the great Cornovii tribe's legendary leaders.

Berrwynn of Burgedin's Story

Told by Silvanus the Unbeliever,
an excommunicated friar from Wycester)

Berrwynn was son of Cadwaladr the then leader of the Powyse/ Cornovii tribe and though named after his grandfather Cadwallon: but referring to his very fair hair he was more popularly known as Berrwynn.

The exiled Celtic Burgedin faction dwelt in an enclosed hilltop fort or Garth and which overlooked the widening Powyse river valley, and near where the great river enters the eastern plains.

Hywel their patron bard romantically referred to its fair location as "As where the goddess Powyse leaves the long and protective arms of Plymon; her mountain god father, and searched a way to her lover, the great ocean god Ceuan y Mor."

Hirwy; her sister river and rival, also craved the love of the ocean god and chose a shorter way to the sea; however Ceuan y Mor preferred Powyse, and the great inrushing 'Severn bore' was his consummation of his love of the goddess.

disinherit Berrwynn deviously contented he untraceably away in war, and probably dead.

The young tribesmen became increasingly impatient by the Cadwaladr family and tribal elders' failure to elect a leader, and demanded Gethinn be their leader. Rhiannon was furious but family members and loyal followers' opposition was overruled, and the popular strong-armed Gethinn, was appointed their new leader.

Initially popular, but when substantiated Gethinn became increasingly dictatorial and was feared and then hated by the populace, and personality change led to much speculation. His sympathisers accused the previous regime's conspiracies was frustrating his rule and compelling him to harshly enforce authority. However opponents cynically construed that Gethinn blamed his loss of eye and other war wounds on Tarran, and he had iniquitously planned that of the wise counselling to gain credibility as compassionate prospective leader.

Gethinn became increasingly insufferable, but Gweneira his wife; and who dearly loved him was prepared to suffer, however when he degenerated into debauchery and amassed concubines from Virconium, it finally broke her heart.

The people also suffered from his inability to dispose balanced justice, and following elder's protestations Gethinn henceforth forbid their involvement in tribal affairs. Rhiannon then approached him expressing her concern that he had and illegally banned the elders, and not receiving credible acceptance she became furiously angry. Thereafter; and of which she later regretted, she impetuously declared that, "During Cadwaladr's rule, and forefathers before him they had never known of such injustices, misrule and such blatant immorality".

Her audacious stinging words infuriated Gethinn and replied that she was only envious of his leadership, and as the

Cadwaladr family members no more held power, she was liable to be tried for treason.

Hywel was fortunate to learn of Gethinn's plans; and knowing he would show no mercy warned Rhiannon of her immanent danger, and with her children and the faithful old bard immediately fled to her sister's home in Pendeva.

For the next five years the family lived in the old Roman fort of Penllyn near Lake Tegid and thus called Tacitus, after a Roman general

Native Ordovices peoples ominously differed from taller and fairer Celts, mostly black haired and swarthy, and testimony of a warmer climate southerly origins.

Berrwynn and sister Aurian happily grew up with their Carrog cousins however Rhiannon's dream was of returning to Burgedin and reclaim the leadership for Berrwynn.

Eventually her dream was fulfilled; but in unexpected way and followed by a most tragic outcome.

THE ORDIVICES CARROG TRIBE OF PENDEVA

The Ordivicis Carrog tribe's people inhabited the lake valley source of the Roman called Deva River and which flowed past their estuary city of Caerdeva

Previous to their Roman conquest Carrog tribe's people resided on crannogs; man made islands ingeniously constructed in the lake and connected by gangways but though defensively constructed they were of no match to the invaders' onslaught.

Beleaguered people fled to remote high valleys and malnutrition through meagre diet substantially reduced their numbers forcing gradual return to Pendeva. But their return was not to traditional crannog existence, but subsistence employment at around the Roman fort at Penllyn.

In the fourth century the Emperor Constantine legislated that Roman citizens become Christian, but enforcing on unwilling natives caused a hostile reaction, and benign local hierarchy allowed non citizens to continue their pagan worship.

Carrog people had previously worshiped a lake serpent goddess called 'Gywer', and believed a snake like driftwood washed on lakeshore was her embodiment, but when fled their island homes they had to abandon their religious image.

It eventually collapsed into the lake and was lost, and re-habituating Pendeva Carrog tribe's people wished to again worship Gywer, and a woodcraftsman tried making a replacement.

Though the carver had expertedly constructed a serpent like body; but lacking visual knowledge of previous image gave the figure a head and similar to an ass. The tribe's people utterly rejected and laughingly referred to it as a legless mule, but such a fine specimen of the woodcarver's skill no one had heart to destroy.

As it somewhat resembled an ass, was altered and sold to the Christian Romans; and unaware of its proposed origin they mounted a figure of their Holy Mother and child on its back. It duly became a much revered holy Christian icon, and thereafter was long preserved in Dervel's church at near Penllyn.

<u>Antonius Maximus</u>

Since end of Roman rule, Pendeva and like many regions became an intermixture of peoples, Carrog tribe's people, Celts and also integrated Romano/Celts and of many other nationalities.

A handsome retaind legionnaire called Antonius Maximus was an answer to many a maiden's dream, and the then very young Rhiannon also secretly fantasised that he some day would maybe notice her.

Antonius however, was aware of her adolescent admiration and was himself captivated by the young black haired beauty, but nearly fifteen years older and a man of honour he considered inappropriate, and ignored her flirtatious gestures.

At the time there occurred a rebellion in Brigantia and Antonius was commanded to assist quell, and becoming seriously wounded he lay for months recovering, and as his whereabouts were unknown he was assumed killed.

Rumoured dead, heartbroken Rhiannon was comforted by young warrior called Cadwaladr, and soon afterwards they married, and with her new husband she moved to his Burgedin home at edge of the great plain.

Whilst lay in his sick bed Antonious's thoughts continually turned to Rhiannon, and he now regretted dismissing her juvenile attentions, and equated as whether fifteen year age difference was that important.

His military career at end, and though in receipt of a pension he brooded over his disabled future, and having made good friends amongst Carrog people he decided that as soon able to travel he would return and ask Rhiannon to marry him.

Antonius became increasingly impatient as to start the journey, but was a long time before came strong enough to accomplish, and when finally arrived in Pendeva he was utterly devastated to discover that Rhiannon had married another.

When Carrog tribe's people learned of his tragic story they felt much sympathy for the wounded Roman and thereafter was made one of their own tribe and he became affectionately known as their Anwar Antwyn or 'The Wounded Anton'.

Re-meeting

When Antonius and widowed Rhiannon again met they delightfully reiterated in their long ago friendships, and similar to when an adolescent maiden long ago she fell again in love with the now grey haired but still handsome legionnaire.

Regaining mature perceptiveness, Rhiannon seriously considered that Antwyn would be an ideal husband and good stepfather to her children. However realised that if they were to marry and were fortunate to return to Burgedin there possibly be tribal opposition.

Pendeva had grown to tolerate the Romans, and though Burgedin was peaceful but as shadowed by their strong neighbour they felt uneasily vulnerable, and without reason mistrusted.

Rhiannon revealed to her trusted mentor Hywel her thoughts of marrying Antwyn and he at first he was surprised and gravely warned of dangers it might imply. But when he considered Antwyn's' honourable reputation and his useful military and administrative skills agreed it could be to their benefit, and then proclaimed, "If Antwyn is also agreeable, the marriage will have also my blessings".

Thereby Rhiannon sent a message inviting Antwyn to visit her sister's house, and curious but naively unaware of the purpose of the invitation he immediately accepted their hospitality.

A customary feast had been laid, and seeing Rhiannon dressed in utmost finery she seemed to him as beautiful as he remembered a long time ago and realised that he was still in love with her.

In course of the feast; and when the wine freely flowed, Rhiannon and fearfully unsure of Antwyn's reaction subtly veiled her suggestion of marriage by asking whether. 'When enough time elapsed since the death of Cadwaladr should she remarry? Naively unaware of significance of her question it confounded Antwyn and he was unable to give a supportable answer.

The following day Hywel approached Antwyn with similar riddle, and suitor still remained naively inarticulate, the old bard and uttering a sigh of exasperation finally and plainly explained "Rhiannon wishes you to marry her".

Antwyn was ecstatic, and unlike the previous time he unhesitatingly proposed marriage, and at the same time sadly reflected that his new acquired happiness had only come through the death of his dear friend Cadwaladr.

The news of the proposed marriage was then released to the Carrog tribe's people and they were delighted for the couple and they wished them a happy future in Pendeva.

It was thought that it was very unlikely that Rhiannon would return to Burgedin and of Berrwyn achieving his rightful inheritance of leadership of the tribe.

After respectful and agonising months of waiting Antwyn and Rhiannon were to be finally married, but as Antwyn was Christian it caused a problem. And it was solved by a combined Christian baptismal and wedding, confirming Rhiannon's only lukewarm acceptance of now Christian faith.

Antwyn's brother Leonidas granted their honeymoon at Caer Gai, the disused fort had been converted to a luxurious villa and where said the Caerdeva Romans' held drunken orgies in the obscurity of the peaceful countryside.

Rhiannon a year later gave birth to twin boys, and were named Gerontius after Antwyn's father and Leonidas after his brother, but Carrog tribe's people referred to them by the Celtic equivalence of Geraint and Llewelyn.

Three years later a girl child was born and she was named Oenone after Anton's Phrygian born mother, but natively unpronounceable was called Onn or Nonn.

The children were of two noticeable strains of parental racial characteristics, firstly Berrwynn was truly Cadwaladr's learned son, and though his sister Aurian had her father's burnished gold hair. She had also inherited the impetuouse nature of her Carrog tribe mother, and earned the title of Aurian Wyllt, or Wild.

Though Geraint and Llewelyn were twins they were totally of opposite characters as chalk from cheese, physically Geraint resembled his Roman father, but as his half sister Aurian also inherited his mother's impetuousness. When young these two siblings were noticeably daring, and in adulthood fearless and were admired as potential leaders by their contemporaries.

Llewelyn however was thoughtful and literate, and his unending thirst of knowledge even exasperated his learned Roman Christian father, and though never wished he was convinced his learned son would eventually become a priest.

Oenone the youngest child whilst physically resembled her mother in having jet black hair and delicate fair skin, was uniquely different from rest of the family.

Oenone had goddess' like mystique inherited from her Greek grandmother and as was ever smiling Hywel affectionately called her Heulwen, meaning Sunshine.

<u>Meanwhile in Burgedin</u>

Whilst their exile in Pendeva there was much unrest in Burgedin, Gethinn in attempting to gain popularity and hopefully unify his people declared war against their old adversary Radyr of Maesyfed. But unknown to him Radyr had long died and his son Llyr or Lear had become their leader, and unlike his father he was a skilled and confident Caerdeva military trained warrior.

Subsequently Gethinn suffered defeat and Burgedin was only saved by their tribal elders pleading Silures friends to threaten invade Maesyfed from the south.

Most people had now grown sorely tired of Gethinn's misrule, and the Cadwaladr followers conspired to reinstate the traditional dynasty but they knew not of how depose such powerful leader. However, when learnt that Rhiannon had married a reputed Roman Legionnaire General the conspirators secretly visited Pendeva and invited Anwar to lead an army against Gethinn.

Though Antwyn had fought in innumerable conflicts it was the first time he faced such a delicate issue, and after a great deal of thought cautiously concluded it be madness to cause deaths and injuries of many of his wife's own tribe's people. Rhiannon's greatest wish was to return to Burgedin and install Berrwynn as their leader but similarly she opposed an armed invasion and cause civil war and of which would poison tribal unity for centuries.

Rumour of an armed invasion by Carrog tribesmen was rife in Burgedin and it caused great fear and also dilemma as to who they sided and fight, and though despised Gethinn they feared for their lives to oppose him.

Gethinn's long-suffering wife Gweneira and fearing the possible results of such a disastrous conflict she pleaded her husband to abdicate leadership, but he ignored her plea as more feared a revengeful aftermath of his own people.

In having no allies Gethinn prepared to commit the unthinkable traitorous action worthy of Gwrthhaearn of Caint who for ever castigated for inviting the overseas Saxons to assist him against a rival Celtic king.

Gethinn planned to bring in the Virconium Legionary Guards to his aid, and his proposal shocked and antagonised his people and they again pleaded Gweneira to define to him the dangers, and try and change his mind.

Gethinn however was not prepared to accept advice, and despairingly Gweneira now contemplated how prevent her husband committing a fate worse than death of displeasing their gods, also own descendants from ever damnable reputation.

Though Gweneira still loved her husband she had now no other option than plan his downfall, and realising only herself was able to get near enough to Gethinn; heartbreakingly contemplated she had to be his assassin.

Acquiring painless poison she prepared for the ultimate action of committing the unthinkable deed of killing the one she loved. The same day; and even before her husband Gethinn had breathed his last breath, the goddess Powyse had already received Gweneira's drowned body.

A bloody civil war averted, and Rhiannon, Antwyn and children were thereafter and wholeheartedly welcomed back to Burgedin, but their reappearance had not solve the leadership problem as Berrwynn was still far too young to be leader.

In the discussions following their return, it was agreed that Rhiannon in having proved of strong personality be installed a temporary leader, but she surprised the elders by declining the roll unless it was joint leadership with her husband.

Traditionalists were unhappy and firstly opposed the Roman, but fearing be again back in their previous position they sought Hywel wise assistance, and he having foreseen the outcome had in his possession a carefully drafted parchment.

His drawn edict contained details of joint leaderships and enforceable stipulation that; as when Berrwynn became of age, or thereafter and when wished, he would be rightfully installed leader of the Burgedin tribal faction.

Following further discussion, and knowing the strength of Rhiannon's personality would ensure Berrwynn's future reign, the tribal elders, and most people whom were tired of continued disagreements it was a solution of leadership they needed.

Thereafter Rhiannon and Antwyn became temporary joint leaders of the tribe and successfully reunited their people.

Rhiannon invited Gethinn and Gweneira's only and now orphaned daughter Marchell to remain in their home in Burgedin, but noticeably Aurian and she; and for some unknown reason became fierce rivals.

Military Training in Caerdeva

Antonius' military connections enabled Berrwynn and his cousin Braan to be enrolled in the Roman Military Academy in Caerdeva, the great Roman City located on Deva estuary.

Their education and in the latin language importantly taught them the arts of war, however suffered taunts of sons of Roman hierarchy referring to native Britons as dirty and uncivilised underlings. Otherwise the two cousins enjoyed much of their stay, worked hard and spent their leisure times riotously drinking and whoring; and the maturing procedure of would be legionnaires.

Though instructed into Roman ways and practices, they and as many other Celtic leaders' sons, remained dutifully true of their roots and their pagan religion, and ingested only what benefited themselves and their tribe's people.

Necessary for hardening future warriors, and at age of seventeen years Berrwynn again left his home to join in the wars, and too young a to seriously bear arms he was employed tending the horses and provisioning food supplies.

On the long journey south accompanied a fresh contingent of mercenary warriors on their way to reinforce his relative the great Tarran of Virconium's army.

Since long ago Buddig of Icena's insurrections, the native population; unless privileged with a Roman connection, were forbidden to bear arms, and when the Roman Legions withdrew were mostly untrained. The now Romano/British cities continued a localised militia, but with no overall control became disorganised and disbanded. Thereafter legionaries such as Tarran sold their military experience fighting the Saxons in the troubled south.

Roman citizens however became concerned of upcoming native Celtic leaders would gain superiority and occupy their Christian cities, and in desperation re-instituted the disbanded legions and were called Legionary Guards.

Veteran Tarran had fought in many battles, and most noted where he commanded a bravely fought campaign defending band of fortified earth forts aligning edge of northern chalk hills. Their Romano/British combined army held the great earth fort or dinn bearing the dragon emblem, but after many successes Tarran was unfortunately wounded and the native forts again fell to the Saxons.

The combined Romano/ Celtic army then retreated to Roman Corinium to assess their losses and re-plan their future strategies.

Berrwynn was too young to be involved in serious bloodshed deserving military honour, however blood relative of the commander he at the age of twenty years proudly bore battle honours. As most young immature men he had great pleasure being admired wearing the battle honours, and could not wait to return home and impress his parents, friends and especially the young maidens of Burgedin.

On learning a number of senior warriors were returning to recruit a substantial number of warriors for then assumed final victory over the Saxons; Berrwynn contemplated was a good opportunity to return home and display his honours.

He request Tarran that he accompany the warriors, and promised he would return with their new intake, and very soon was joyfully on his way home to Burgedin, - proudly bearing his valiant honours.

Chapter III

<u>Tresoara</u>

Berrwynn arrives in Burgedin. Adoration to frustration. Travels to Pendeva, and he again meets' the lovely Tresoara. They elope and hide in their hidden valley and tey meet the bard/shepherds. Winter approaches and they prepare to leave.

Berrwynn was indeed a war hero to the Burgedin tribe's people and he arrived home to a tremendous welcome by multitude of admirers, his mother Rhiannon, brothers, sisters, stepfather and elders awaited in line to warmly embrace him.

Hywel their patron bard had composed a poem commemorating his bravery, and a great celebration feast was prepared for him, and where drank, sang and danced until exhausted at dawn.

As their future leader, Berrwynn's attention was now constantly sought by all the marriageable young maidens and even more by ambitious parents, but in now having achieved physical maturity began to revel in their pleasures.

When Rhiannon manipulatively proposed that Marchell be his wife Berrwynn was outraged and refused; and gentle maid having come to truly love the young warrior was deeply hurt.

Berrwynn also caused dismay amongst the tribe's people when also declined his immediate leadership, and further offended when flippantly replied that he was mostly too drunk to administer justice; - and ironically, it was probably true.

However his rejection of marriage prospects only increased his allure and more maidens hopeful clamoured his attention, and in becoming relentless it eventually irritated him. Unbelievably, after his initial glorification; the vain honour bearing peacock now wished a quieter life and too enjoy the company of his friends, and more importantly choose his own female companions.

After the few hectic months at his home, Berrwynn was relieved when invited by his cousin Braan to stay the summer at his home in Pendeva, and immediately packed his belongings and headed there along their usual Tannat route.

When Marchell learned that Berrwynn had departed for Pendeva she was further hurt, and sorely dejected also left Burgedin travelling with a passing mule train to Maesyfed, and a long time elapsed before she was heard of again.

Amongst Carrog Tribe.

Arriving in Pendeva Berrwynn was again celebrated by his Carrog tribe relatives, and when again met Braan's younger sister Tresoara he was surprised that since he last seen she had blossomed from a frail young girl to an exceptional beauty.

He was entranced by her shapely slim figure and exceptionaly glorious ebony hair which hung down to her waist and enhancing her soft white complexion and before long the two became inseparable

Pendeva being cradle of the bards they attended all their merry gatherings, danced until tired then sang endearing songs to the harp or listened to the bards telling tales late into the night by the fireside.

Tresoara's father when young man had served Cynddelw the King of Gwydyr and achieving military distinction earned the name of Blaidd or Wolf of Gwydyr. When the Carrog leader died without sons to succeed Blaidd was invited to marry his eldest daughter Colwen and subsequently installed their leader.

Colwen bore him five sons in succession and desperate for a daughter he pleaded their god Arran, and in accord granted their wish, and deisticaly grateful Blaidd gave her the name of Tresoara, and femininely meaning 'Gift of Arran'.

Secretly, Tresoara had always loved her three year older cousin Berrwynn, and noticeably at beginning of every summer excitedly awaited his arrival, but when he later departed was sad and tearful.

When again met the now physically matured and handsome warrior; Tresoara experienced feelings previously unknown to her, and she obsessively sought all opportunities to be with him. Her love of Berrwynn was known to her mother and though not openly encouraged neither hindered, but as Braan also enjoyed his cousin's company the lovers had little time alone. Sympathetically Colwen often sent Braan on fool's errands, in so much that Tresoara and Berrwynn could be together.

Blaidd and envious of Cynddelw's great wealth ambitiously betrothed his daughter Tresoara to his eldest; but effeminate son Crwys, and in that one day she be Queen of Gwydyr. But when Blaidd learned of his daughter association with Berrwynn he desperately tried to discourage, and though throughout her young life unquestionably accepted her father's will. But now older and inheriting her father's strong mind blatantly disregarded his wishes.

Mighty Blaidd was not usually a one to be disobeyed, but even he found hard to deny his loving daughter, however he considered Tresoara too immature as to appreciate her great future prospects. And he then tried to entice her by quoting the immense riches of Gwydyr, of its gold, copper, lead and silver mines and trade to Cernwy, Ireland, and even as far north as Alban.

However; it was to no avail, and realising his dreams were in jeopardy forbid his daughter to meet or even to speak to Berrwynn, but in spite of strong paternal pressure the two clandestinely met in woods lining the shores of Llyn Tegid.

If only Blaidd could have foreseen that Crwys was never to rule Gwydyr, as the prince's unnatural preferences caused him to suffer traditional nose disfigurement and disposed, and thereafter his younger brother Llewelyn succeeded him as king.

Berrwynn and Tresoara's clandestine assignments ended when vagabond thieves sheltering in the woods accidentally discovered the lovers, and sensing a reward their odious leader Gardo approached Blaidd with the incriminating story.

The following day Berrwynn was informed that he was no longer welcomed in Pendeva and devastatingly advised to return to Burgedin, and wishing to bid Tresoara farewell he searched all usual meeting places but he could not locate.

It was only by a chance meeting with traitorous Gardo and handsomely bribing him did Berrwynn discover that Tresoara had been sent at night by boat to Caer Gai; a Roman fort at far end of the lake, and was detained there by relatives.

Thoroughly despondent Berrwynn was in quandary as whether to immediately return home without seeing Tresoara or find her and bid her a last farewell. At no time did he consider rescuing her, as making an enemy of mighty Blaidd was a very serious matter and of which could lead the tribes into a bloody war.

The scheming road thief leader suggested to Berrwynn that if he encircled the lake he could reach Caer Gai unobserved in a few hours, and hoping to speak to his love heeded Gardo, and they laboriously trekked the lake's long southern shore.

When the evening light faded Berrwynn quietly approached the villa and peeked through shuttered windows searching for signs of his love. Tresoara had a little black and white dog called D'wyn, and it was its recognisable sharp bark which alerted Berrwynn as where slept. But it being an above room it was difficult to gain entry, and solved by improvising a branched log as ladder. Awakened by the commotion Tresoara arose from her bed and approached the window carrying barking Dwyn. When saw Berrwynn clinging to a swaying log ladder she immediately held the little dog's nose to prevent it from further barking and awaken the whole household.

In seeing Berrwynn Tresoara was overjoyed, and considered he must truly love her by him risking his life rescuing her in defiance of her father Blaidd, but knew not he had only come to bid her a last farewell.

But when Berrwynn saw her slender form silhouetted through her thin nightshift he became ecstatically enthralled and befuddled his prepared farewell speech. However in her relief of seeing him Tresoara in her excitement was oblivious to his garbled words, and sobbingly called that she loved him and pleaded him to take her away, and that she never ever wanted to see her father again.

His sudden onset of passion clouded Berrwynn's mind of all reason and was again in a quandary, and Gardo sensing an opportunity of gaining even more lucre deviously suggested a solution. He revealed that amongst mountains north of Caer Gai he had a well stocked hideout located near a tarn and which teemed with fish and wild ducks and geese were also abundant.

Gardo sensed Tresoara was interested in his hideout, and not allowing Berrwynn time to dissuade hurriedly added, that he; and at a reasonable price, would lead the young couple to the hidden fold in the mountains.

On Tresoara's insistence the offer was accepted, and after warmly dressing she gathered up her belongings and they crept quietly away through the woods. Gardo leading the way and followed by the lovers carrying Dwyn and with nose bound with her mistress' hair ribbon to prevent her barking.

After hours of strenuous climbing and constant tripping over objects in the dark the dawn broke and weak sun shone through red clouds in the east, and then on could see their way.

The surrounding hillside was barren and strewn with giant boulders offering numerous dry clefts and that could easy hide an army. Eventually they came upon a high cwm and at its centre a small dark lake encircled by reeds and a few trees.

Tresoara was near collapsed with hunger and exhaustion, and Berrwynn insisted Gardo to immediately lead them to his hidden hideout, and turned out to be a natural cleft. It had however a stone built front, wooden door and a shuttered window, and staggering inside they surprisingly found the dwelling dry and warm and along its side had racks with sheep fleeces and obviously meant to be beds.

From a slated cavity Gardo produced pieces of scarcely eatable cheese however was immediately relished, afterwards the tired travellers laid down where could and in the serene safety of the high valley exhaustedly slept for many hours.

Berrwynn awoke to the sound of Dwyn's sharp bark, and lying motionless he cast his eyes around the dim shack lit only by the sunrays shinning through cracks in wooden shuttered window.

Casting his eyes sidewise he observed Tresoara still in land of dreams but Gardo's bed place was vacated, and the same time he sensed a movement near where they had disorderly deposited their possessions on arrival.

Peering into the gloom he saw a human figure kneeling over their packs, and from Tresoara's pack extracting glittering objects and consigning into a pouch at his waist. The thief then began searching the remaining packs, and subsequently Berrwynn's coveted silver coins were tucked into the rapidly filling pouch, and enraged Berrwynn leaped out of his bed to apprehend.

However the disturbance alerted the thief and he ran towards the door, but it also caused Dwyn to excitedly run around barking and obstructed Berrwynn's path, and by now he recognised it was Gardo. The thief escaped out of the shack, and Berrwynn barefooted painfully pursued along a rocky path, and unable to catch he was tempted as to throw his sword at the thief. However sensibly realised, that if missed his target, could possibly reward the thief a weapon and whilst he be then weapon-less himself.

The only path zigzagged down a steep hill and alongside Berrwynn noticed heap of rocks, holding a large rock above his head he waited until Gardo was directly beneath. Venting his anger he heaved the jagged rock at the thief, and though he had had no pre-conceived intention of killing Gardo, but the gods intervened and guided its jagged edge at the thief's vulnerable neck and causing his instant death.

Berrwynn was shocked when realised, that he; and for the first time killed a man, but subsequently laid aside any guilt feelings as judged his demise was a justified punishment instigated by the gods, in that they had guided the fatalistic rock.

In not wishing to appear a bloodthirsty avenger he decided to keep Gardo's death a secret from Tresoara and carefully searched for a place to bury the body, but it left him in a quandary as the ground to hard and insufficient loose rocks to cover.

Not far away lay the lake and lifting Gardo's lifeless body on his shoulder he made his way towards, but on the way he spotted a hollow tree and with a cavity large enough to hide a body.

Congratulating himself on his ingenuity he lowered Gardo's slender body into the hollow trunk and then covered the opening with a few stones and turf, and he then made his way to the shack bearing retrieved stolen goods. Riches he found in Gardo's own pouch surprised him, as included several gold coins and of which were ever hardly seen outside confines of Roman hierarchy's purses.

On reaching the shack's door he politely knocked as not catch Tresoara unawares and cause embarrassment, and was cheerfully summoned to enter and discovered her standing by a table preparing a meal and obviously unaware of recent events.

Whilst warmly embracing, Berrwynn noticed over her shoulder that the meal was laid for three persons, and he realised that he had quickly to invent a convincing story to explain non-appearance of Gardo. His first task was to covertly return to her pack the retrieved gold chain and six silver bangles before she discovered missing, and he was able whilst she fetched water from nearby stream.

When sat for the meal Berrwynn casually mentioned that he had paid Gardo and he had returned to Pendeva, but then realised he had made a fundamental mistake as news of Gardo's return alarmed the astute Tresoara. Hastily she inferred that the murderous thief could not be trusted, and as on his return he would obviously sell his knowledge of their whereabouts to her father.

Unable to find an alternative satisfactory explanation inn which to lay her fears, Berrwynn realised that lying to the intelligent Tresoara was futile, and concluded he had no other option than tell her the truth.

"My dearest", he said "I confess; have lied to you, and I promise that never again will hide secrets from you, and sincerely hope you will forgive me for deceiving you".

Tresoara was deeply touched by Berrwynn's heartfelt plea of forgiveness, and though immensely curious temporarily withheld her questioning and instead fell into his arms. And he tasted her salty tears as he passionately kissed her rosy lips.

A considerable time later whilst lying close together on the warm sheep fleece by the fire Tresoara unfettered her feminine inquisitiveness and whispered in his ear. "My dearest Berrwynn, and as by natural laws you are now my husband, will you not now tell what you had earlier to confess, and whatever the offence I have thus already proved my forgiveness".

Berrwynn revealed to her what had really occurred, and that he had lied to protect her from distressing thoughts of bloodshed, and also had not wished of her to regard his action of him merely avenging Gardo for his thieving.

He now realised Tresoara was of a strong character when then declared, "Though; as you say the deed was an accident, however it has solved our problem" and aware of Gardo's murderous reputation added. "If had not occurred, we would have had to take remedial action to safeguard our anonymity".

Now that the traitorous informer Gardo was silenced, the young couple could safely stay hidden, but Berrwynn secretly kept ever vigil of intruders in the valley, as the thief's absence might attract fellow thieves searching for him.

In having no priest to officiate a ceremony, and wishing uphold ancient betrothal traditions the much in love young couple firstly bathed in the tarn and thereafter Tresoara carefully combed her hair and dressed herself in her best apparel.

Hoping their ignorance would not displease the gods, individually they entered a copse and Berrwynn cut an oak branch and Tresoara a holly branch and were entwined with ivy strand to confirm their unity. As tradition they dipped the bonded garland in the tarn waters for blessings of the goddess of fertility, and not knowing what else they finally left displayed on a boulder for Arran's blessing.

<u>The Bards, Davad and 'Roen</u>

A few days later they became alarmed when observed two figures sitting on the hillside, and too late to retreat unseen they had no other option than approach the strangers. Were much relieved however to discover they were shepherds from a distant farm, and Berrwynn chastised himself for not before realising that the grazing sheep and goats were obviously someone's property.

Though the senior shepherd revealed their names he related that his acquaintances called him Davad as to a wart on his face; and as 'davad' also means sheep he found amusingly appropriate. Furthermore was inevitable his broad shouldered son was thereafter similarly called 'Roen, and meaning 'The Lamb'.

Berrwynn was surprised that they were unperturbed by the derogatory names; and he was reluctant to address them as so, however he was proud of his own acquired name. Meaning 'Fairhead' and relating to his Celtic descent, and satisfyingly opposite to the Romans', having mostly black hair and darker skin

Davad revealed he had long ago come from Gwydyr with Blaidd as his bard, and growing tired of his constant rages; he and for a more peaceful life left his services and carved out a small mountain farm out of the wilderness.

Berrwynn and Tresoara soon became good friends with the shepherds and spent many idle hours conversing with them on heather clad hillsides or when rained by their fireside in their cosy peat build 'hafod'; their summer pastures' shack.

Fire Gardo had lit them they had negligently left to die and without knowledge of rekindling lacked the necessary means for cooking and warmth, and learning of their predicament the shepherds gave them a perforated clay pot. It allowed them preserve embers by periodically added dry moss and twigs and to readvicate as to inflame; by blowing through a blowhole.

Whilst watching flocks Davad spent much time composing poetry and songs and periodically sold to travelling bards, and Berrwynn were truly amazed at the shepherds' composing capacity and of their epic story telling. And as he had enjoyed listening to Hywel's tales were now entertained by the shepherds' endless mythical stories of gods and goddesses.

Davad's related of the ever placid Deva River goddess, and who when sadly parted from her husband Arran shed immense tears and thus formed Llyn Tegid. Others were of the sun god Grian and whom ruled by day, and moon god Gelach whom ruled the night, both of these gods competed for the favours of the most beautiful goddess of all; our earth goddess Talam.

The two major gods; and like canines harassing a bitch, one by day and other by night courted by continually encircling the beautiful great earth goddess Talam.

Sun god never once wavered from beaming his warm rays, whilst rival Moon god smiled on the earth goddess only periodically. The rest of the time turned his dark back searching the universe for other lovers, and inevitably it was the sun god's warmth which mostly won Talam's heart.

Talam however bore both lovers many sons and daughters; minor deities of rivers and mountains, and those fathered by sun god Grian were benevolent, but the fewer by Gelach the moon god were apt to be evil.

Amongst others Talam also bore twin sons, and uniquely were only half-brothers, and one fathered by Grian was called Arran, and the other by Gelach called Duaran, and since conception they were bitter rivals.

The twin gods competed for love of Deva the river goddess, and Arran inheriting Grian's comforting warmth won her heart, and Duaran was bitterly jealous until eventually found another, the river goddess Mawddwy.

Mawddwy was a lively and happy goddess, but soon got tired of Duaran's dark moods, and unlike placid Deva she hastened to escape her husband, by choosing the shortest route to the sea, and in her haste continually flooded.

Berrwynn and Tresoara enjoyed Davad's mythological tales, and when once he praised; Roen proudly proclaimed his much travelled father was also the most knowledgeable of all the surrounding mountain tracks.

Berrwynn reflected that his geographical knowledge could be very useful if he possibly needed guidance of a way to escape from Blaidd and his warriors.

Shortly after the young couple's arrival in the valley a little white mountain-pony followed and nibbled Tresoara's hair and seemed it was seeking human affection, and referring to her colour called the pony Gwen.

When opportune, Tresoara asked Davad who owned the pony, but he knew not, but informed it had been there for a considerable time, and was most probably abandoned by Gardo's road thieves.

Throughout the glorious summer months Berrwynn and Tresara spent their time in conjugal bliss in their own little paradise constantly making love, swimming in the tarn and lazily laying for hours in the sun. They also hunted, fished or happily roamed the hills with Tresoara riding the little pony she had fallen in love with and when inclement they retreated to the cosy shack listened to the rain battering against the shuttered window.

So happy and contented they never contemplated that their honeymoon would ever end and they hardly noticed the passing of the seasons, and after blissful warm months of summer now dawned had now face the prospect of a cold winter.

The winter weather was approaching and the shepherds were already gathering their sheep for lowland wintering, however momentary were still able to fish in the lake and kill an occasional duck, but soon they would fly away for the winter.

The departure of the shepherds also meant the end of their regular supply of milk and also cheese and other commodities brought by Davad's wife from the farm, and without these facilities they could not possibly survive.

Realising they could not stay at this high altitude and suffer the cold and hunger throughout the winter they now and urgently discussed their future, and following continued altered plans they finally decided to return to the warmer lowlands.

But as Penllyn settlement was in between they asked of their knowledgeable friend Davad of the best route to avoid encountering Blaidd.

As Roen had predicted Davad knew of another way but warned it was fraught with danger; travelling over mountains towards a lonely sunless valley and whose waters flowed oppositely to the western sea.

Continuing in his slow and deliberate speech advised "On no account descend into a foreboding valley shadowed under the dark Duaran mountain as inhabited by extremely hostile dwarf peoples. Called Red Quillons, as from head to feet are covered in reddish hair, they awkwardly walk on two long feet, and are said to talk as do humans. Tales are told that they first appeared after was seen a fire ball in the sky emitting black smoke as it disappeared with thunderous roar over the mountains."

Berrwynn was unsure whether Davad stated facts or was again engrossed in spinning mythical tales, however allowed the shepherd to continue. "Along a summit path you will discover a cairn of stones, and there follow an eastern leading track leading to yet another valley, and which is source of a major river."

Peculiar to Davad; after further thought he changed his mind adding "As you have been my good friends throughout the summer; and as be sure that you choose the correct way, Roen will escort you as far as the cairn, - but no further".

The next few days Berrwynn and Tresoara planned and prepared for the journey but dared not attempt without a sign from their god Arran giving his blessing, and anxiously they waited for his expected sign signalling the start their journey.

One very sultry night there struck an extraordinary flash of lightening and was followed by a tremendous thunderbolt and of which echoed from peak to peak and rocking their shelter. The usual dawn cackling of water fowl and the sky larks singing completely ceased and the valley remained eerily silent, and in their warm bed Tresoara clung to Berrwynn in fear.

Further in the morning the sun again shone in the sky and the lovers with arms entwined gazed down at the little valley below, and subsequently became aware of sweet aroma of burning wood.

Alarmed; and suspecting that they might have unwelcome visitors invading their nest Berrwynn went to investigate, and when returned found Tresoara had barricaded herself in the shack.

Laughing, he called out for her to open the door and revealed cause of the fire was that of the old oak hulk containing Gardo's dead body struck by lightening and completely incinerated.

Looking at the charred remains they were now convinced it was Arran's sign of his approval and it was now time to start their journey.

That very evening they sadly bid their farewell to the enchanted cwm and where they had so much enjoyed their blissful time together. Leading the fully laden pony down the zigzag path neither looked backwards; and pledged that when became old they would once again visit together.

CHAPTER IV

RETURN JOURNEY

They leave their enchanted cwm. Crossing mist ridden mountain pass Berrwynn falls and meets Quillons. They arrive in Pen-Avernwy, and fear of cannibals. Escape, and meet the Christian fishermen. They tiredly finally arrive in Maifod.

As the sun began to set over mountains to the west Berrwynn and Tresoara led the little pony carrying their belongings down the zigzagging mountain track towards Caer Gai.

When reached vicinity of the villa it was safely dark but as a further precaution decided to give it a wider berth compelling them to cross a brook recently swollen by the storm. Thoroughly wet, they had now to endure an uncomfortable cold trek to the little valley as described by the shepherds as the location of their farm. Following a muddy track they eventually came to a ramshackle farmstead.

Though it was now very late they were warmly welcomed by Davad and his wife and amply fed whilst their clothes were dried by a roaring fire, thereafter; and besides their protestations, their hosts insisted they sleep in their vacated bed.

Early the following morning they were again fed a delicious meal of cold mutton and goat's milk cheese, and provided also with provisions for continuance of the journey ahead. And as soon were ready to start they bid their hosts farewell, and guided by the reliable Roen they began ascending the track leading over the bleak mist shrouded mountain pass.

It was a strenuous climb to the summit and it was now they fully appreciated the willing services of Gwen the little pony carrying their belongings, and because of swirling mist causing poor visibility it was midday before reached the summit. Berrwynn was pleased that the track's hard stony surface still continued, as the mountain plateaus are usually notorious for their dangerous bogs.

After endless trudge along the mist ridden summit, Roen revealed that a short distance ahead was 'pen' of the dark mysterious valley described as where the red ogres dwelled, and fortunately was thickly hidden by mist.

As not to attract attention they there on proceeded extremely quiet and nervously listening for sounds excluding from below, and described by Davad as sounding like screeching cats in the night. Thankfully they heard nothing of ogres, and the only sounds they heared was the fast thumping of their own fearful hearts.

Soon out of the mist there loomed the stone cairn and an eastwards leading track that they had now to follow, and resting at foot of the cairn they were extremely thankful that they had safely arrived without encountering the ogres.

Sadly, they had now to part with Roen and continue the journey alone, and before his departure Tresoara presented him with one of her silver bangles, and though protested that he need not be rewarded, he was finally persuaded to accept. Berrwynn however advised him not immediately trade as he might be accused of its theft, and instead save until he had an opportunity to speak to Braan of Carrog. "Show him the bangle, and reveal his sister is well, and by your action he will see you are honest and truthful and he will also reward you".

After bidding a sorrowfully farewell Roen turned away and rapidly disappeared into the swirling mist, and after his departure Berrwynn and Tresoara helplessly felt alone, and very anxious to descend from the frightful mist covered summit.

Though anxious to fast proceed they had to cautiously negotiate eastern track's even steeper gradient, and the further they travelled the more the track twisted and turned. Suddenly the track ended, and without a path and mist obstructing the sun they became disoriented, and leading Gwen the pony along a ridge Berrwynn stumbled and disappeared and into what Tresoara feared was oblivion.

Tresoara frantically called his name until her throat ached and with no response her first reaction was to search for him, but realised it was too dangerous in such diminished visibility. Instead tethered Gwen to a boulder and clutching Dwyn to her breast tearfully awaited the mist to clear, but as time past she became increasingly despondent.

Contemplated that even if the mist cleared she and alone could not find her way, however without Berrwynn she had no wish to leave or live. Her clothes now soaked through sitting in wet heather she prayed to Arran, but feeling become unresponsive earnestly prayed to any diety in their vicinity for Berrwynn's safety.

Laying in a rock strewn hollow Berrwynn's head throbbed from hard impact and he became aware of approaching voices, and assuming it was Tresoara he called out that he was gratefully alive. But when whom spoke neared he realised they were strangers, and outlined against mist penetrating sunlight stood two small people, and unable to move he again called on them to rescue him.

Too late, Berrwynn now realised that they were the dreaded ogres whom Davad had warned him and for sake of his life to avoid.

He strangely noticed that though the creatures spoke in a screechy manner their language was partly understandable as his own.

In discovering Berrwynn lying helpless with a swollen bleeding head, the female of the two ogres benevolently made a poultice of sodden peaty moss and placed on the swelling and its sheer coldness considerably eased his pain.

Berrwynn was most surprised and he was extremely grateful of their kindness, and eventually he was able to sit up against a boulder and drink a little water they also gave him.

He now tried to profoundly thank them, and hearing his voice the dwarfs' faces appeared to kindly smile, and finding them friendly and he curious of their strange lives began to question them.

The ogres complied by revealing their names were Drog and Eagog, and as they had inherited more than usual human genes traits of decency and mercy they had been hounded by those of them whom held only the raw animal instincts. Thereon they escaped to this inhospitable mountain wilderness, living in a cave, and further stressed that in being between two enemies was extremely difficult. As they not only feared encountering their own kind, but also humans and who precautionary killed all their kind.

During their conversation the mist was slowly lifting and a while later was heard a dog's sharp bark, the dwarfs disappeared as if by magic and Berrwynn began to wonder whether he had only imagined their presence.

In finding him; the excitable Dwyn pounced upon him and Berrwynn's face was affectionately licked, and following the sound of the barking Tresoara cautiously descended into the hollow and seeing Berrwynn was alive she cried tears of joy.

They sat there warmly embracing until Berrwynn felt able to continue the journey, and recovering Gwen still tied to a boulder, and he with information the ogres had given, they were gratefully restored to the former path.

Descending with utmost care they soon came out of the summit mist and into glorious sunshine, and extremely hungry eat the food the shepherds had provided, and whilst they rested Berrwynn began relating of his meeting with the ogres. But Tresoara only laughed and intimated it was an illusion he attained by being concussed. Her lover now safe she was now extremely happy and continuously giggled at the dirty peat running down Berrwynn's face and with no clean water to wash had he no other option than happily bear her mirth.

Presently they saw far below a pleasant valley and in the distance they glimpsed a wisp of smoke spiralling upwards, and further descending revealed it came from a few scattered huts, and as evening was approaching they increased their speed.

On reaching the valley floor they saw a river and assumedly it was the one they had to follow, but decided firstly to visit the settlement in hope of attaining food and possibly also a bed for oncoming night.

Firstly they had to cross the river, and provided Berrwynn with his much needed wash to rid the ludicrous peat, and reaching the opposite bank spotted embedded in the clay a grotesque human skull. Secretly musing that it was a bad omen, and distracting Tresoara he discreetly kicked the skull into the river and quickly sank.

Whilst distantly approached the settlement children came running towards them, but their parents, and possibly alarmed swiftly drove back into the compound.

Nearing the settlement Berrwynn stopped dead in his track when observed what had had thought a tree was figure of a man made from rushes. He was reminded of when educated by Romans was told of the horrific tales of human sacrifices practised by druids concerning straw like made human figures.

When they arrived at the settlement the tribe's people stood armed awaiting their arrival, but when they perceived that the travellers were unarmed they cautiously welcomed them in the old dialect.

In questioning their mission, Berrwynn explained they were a humble couple travelling east to escape the worst of the winter weather.

Their leader named Argor, assured them they were at the source of the Avernwy River, and also affirmed it eventually flowed into a greater river.

He proclaimed that when saw them descending the mountain track and crossing the valley towards their settlement feared they were a party of Quillans and hurriedly reached for their weapons.

Though claimed the Quillans were rarely seen nevertheless were fierce and no member of their tribe would venture the way they had approached the valley, and reflected was fortunate the summit was covered by mist. Otherwise he doubted they would have survived, as whoever encountered the ogres had never survived to convey their experience.

In Berrwynn enquiring of their tribe, Argor inferred they had long dwelled in this high isolated valley and rarely saw strangers, and added it was a blessing as their unknown existence afforded them no enemies, except maybe the Quillans.

But when Berrwynn asked about the great wicker and rushes figure, Argor said it represented Taan the fire god and burned as to celebrate his arrival amongst them.

Somewhat apologetically Argor informed that their people were very poor and could offer them very little hospitality, but welcomed them to share what little they had.

When Tresoara observed the people was shocked at their poverty and sickliness, their faces were dull and ragged garb hung on their gaunt bodies, but it was the undernourished state of the children which brought her the most sorrow.

A while later Tresoara began to feel uncomfortable when noticed the tribesmen continually gazing at her and Berrwynn with hungry looks in their eyes, and her imagination began to rule her mind. She became extremely alarmed and struggled to overcome fears that to satisfy their hunger tribe's people adopted cannibalism.

Berrwynn meanwhile had his back to her talking to the leader and was unaware of her anxiety, and the extremely tensed Tresoara clutched his arm and dragged him aside and whispered her worst fears. He however was much surprised at her concern and smiled, but when he again turned to face the garb ridden hungry crowd he sympathised with her concern.

Though Berrwynn had heard of cannibalism was not convinced existed and believed were myths, or otherwise lies purported by opposing tribes of their enemies. However he put his arm around Tresoara to reassure his protection, and not confronted such situation before he thought was wiser to stay alert, and though was unlikely correct, cautionary made plans as to protect themselves.

Firstly he advocated that Tresoara stay at his side at all times and remain alert of any signs of the tribesmen attempting to capture them. Grasping hilt of his sword beneath his garb and with his other hand covertly passed Tresoara his dagger to conceal under her tunic, whilst solemnly added. "If becomes necessary, do not hesitate to use".

Thinking back what Davad had said of their journey of 'being fraught with danger' he now wondered whether referred to ogres or to a cannibalistic tribe, and began to question whether they were the friends he had imagined them to be.

Invited inside the largest hut for a meal and on entering they observed roasting above a fire a skewed thin carcass, and an animal Berrwynn could not recognise. When Tresoara saw the white meat she was petrified and acclaimed it was surely human flesh, but Berrwynn was still unconvinced and reminding her of their impoverishment he stated that the roasting carcass was probably a fox or a dog.

In him mentioning dog; Tresoara instinctively clutched her little dog against her breast, and equally terrified proclaimed that on no account would tomorrow's meal be her little Dwyn.

Thoughtfully, Berrwynn secretly mused; might not be the dog Dwyn - but us.

The roasting meat smelt delicious, and though extremely hungry the pair had no stomach for the tribesmen's delicacy, and when invited to partake they politely declined, saying they had already eaten.

Whilst the meal was being eaten the pair crept out of the dimly fire lit hut and into the now completely dark exterior, and worried of the fate of Gwen their little pony they were relived to find unharmed, and still harnessed was quietly grazing.

Gathering their belongings they stealthily made their way down the valley and anxiously glancing over their shoulders whenever heard or any imagined sounds.

However the more miles gained between themselves and the tribesmen - the less Berrwynn thought that they were cannibals.

Following the twisting river, and when entered a woody ravine they had difficulty negotiating its steep banks, and now ravenously hungry but also very tired and finding a dry dell they halted for the night. Cosily wrapped in two sown together fleeces they settled down for the night under the stars, and thanked benevolent gods for kindly withholding the rain.

Extreme hunger caused them to awake as soon as the daylight penetrated through the overhanging trees, and Berrwynn discussed catching fish to eat, but unhappily discovered their coveted fire carrier negligently extinguished and unable to cook.

Whilst Tresoara washed in the river Berrwynn searched for anything consumable but found only crab apples and of which Tresoara vehemently refused to eat, and weak of lack of subsidence they and wearily continued their journey.

After exiting the barely penetrable woody ravine the valley widened and further they travelled the greater became the river from innumerable small tributaries, and soon the river became too deep to safely ford.

Having travelled a considerable distance Berrwynn contemplated that they were now probably out of Arran's influence and he hoped an unknown to them god, was as also as benevolent to their plight. "More likely it be a river goddess" Tresoara replied, and truly it was granted, rounding a river bend they came across fishermen sitting around a fire consuming deliciously smelling cooked salmon.

Thanking benevolent god; or maybe Tresoara's predicted river goddess, they approached the fishermen offering a coin for the fish, and their only meal since the previous day it was most enjoyable.

Kind heartedly, Tresoara shared her meal with Dwyn, and as not to appear selfish Berrwynn likewise and the tiny dog happily consumed a third share of the meal.

Thereafter conversing on the river bank the fishermen confirmed the Avernwy flowed into the Mother River; namely of the goddess Powyse, and contradictorily added that they no longer believed in the ancient gods and goddesses.

As wise men from afar had baptised them in a holy well and henceforth they worshiped a one deity and who magically divided into three, and that they were now immortal. Another of the fisherman interrupted saying that only their souls were immortal, as the god once died and then arose and walked on the water to Ierland But the third; and the oldest declared that was nonsense as the great god lives in an enormous hut and he has a shepherds' crook and a gold helmet.

Further conversations with the fishermen revealed the wise men only lived six Roman miles down the valley, and had build a large house of stones as refuge for whoever seeks protection from wrath of pagan gods, and whom do not exist.

Berrwynn and Tresoara were confused by their bizarre explanations of their new beliefs and whilst continued their journey along the pleasant valley they contemplated the intriguing and also amusingly contradictory fishermen's stories.

In their hearts they were now full of curiosity; but as not to anger their recently acquired patron 'goddess of the Avernwy', they pre cautionary declared that they wholeheartedly believed in the power of their ancient gods.

Towards the evening they encountered another tributary and seeing a lone hunter on the opposite bank Berrwynn hailed and enquired how far it was to wise men's house of sanctuary. He replied it was two Roman miles away and fortunately it was on the same side of the river that they were presently travelling.

The hunter also called out to them that the wise men were extremely benevolent and provided hungry travellers with food and bed as long as they listened to their teachings. Though he warned, beware they may possibly offer to baptise you in a spring called holy, but firstly wiser to ask their own gods approval; as not anger.

After seemingly hours of walking along the river bank and in rounding a copse they finally viewed but somewhat disappointedly a reed roofed stone building enclosed within remains of a stone circle.

In the fast failing light they felt uneasy approaching the unlit gloomy building and where not a living soul was anywhere to be seen, and in trying the door Berrwynn found was barred.

Tresoara then nervously reminded him to first ask the river goddess' approval, and returning to the riverside they discarded their footwear and stood knee deep in the icy water shivering awaiting a sign of goddess' acknowledgement.

Their long cold awaited response was none too soon when eventually came with a distinct splash.

It seems their presence had disturbed an otter, and the shivering pair hurriedly exited the cold river only half convinced heard sounds was the river goddess' sign of approval.

For the second time Berrwynn and Tresoara approached the wise men's stone house of sanctuary, and wondered whether they would be welcomed.

They were now very tired, extremely cold and also again hungry and they dared not contemplate what they would do if were turned away.

Fig 3 The Maifod Mission

Chapter V

The Christian Brothers

Berrwynn and Tresoara meet the wise men called Christian Brothers. They learn of the Christian faith and Tresoara is converted but Berrwynn is sceptical and resists. Tresoara announces that she is pregnant with child.

Berrwynn knocked on the stone house' door but brought no response, knocking harder and augmented by Dwyn's incessant barking there came sounds of shuffling footsteps and undistinguished mutterings. Then came a querulous voice enquiring; "Who's calling at this unearthly hour?" the response surprised the travellers as it was only little after sunset and normal time for feasting.

Bolts were then heard drawn and the door was slightly opened and a pale drawn face peaked out, and Berrwynn immediately proclaimed that they were travellers and in dire need of food and bed for the night.

His plea brought a grunt and the door was opened a little wider; and illuminated by a flickering candle stood a gaunt figure and obviously irritated because of his disturbed sleep. For a while he studied the late callers, and Berrwynn suspecting he was about to refuse them charity hurriedly proclaimed that he was able to pay, and only then did the figure stand aside and allow their entry.

No sooner Berrwynn and Tresoara had stepped inside than he announced his name was Cadfan, and was a Christian; and aiming to convert to his religion he began telling its history. In that was brought to these shores by Romans, and Padriag in Iwerddon; meaning Ireland, had commanded his father Brychan, a mission to convert all remaining Britons into their one true religion'.

The tired and hungry travellers' immediate concern however was of fulfilling their physical needs, and eventually Berrwynn had to interrupt Cadfan's monologue, by asking as where was the food? And in him repeating the offer of a silver coin brought a desired result.

They were led to a chamber and where the dying embers still glowed on a stone hearth and paying their host Berrwynn and Tresoara sat down by a rekindled fire. Cadfan and out of the darkness brought them cold pork and a jug of earthy beer, and before exiting informed they could sleep the night in this warm chamber called kitchen.

When eaten and thereafter discovering some empty flour sacks they very tiredly settled down for a long night's sleep; or so they had thought, as before dawn they were awakened by loud chanting.

It became even worse when the wise men came into the kitchen to start prepare the morning meal, dragging tables along the stone floor and noisily clattering of pans whilst still chanted, and Dwyn also began howling to their accompaniment.

Berrwynn and Tresoara were unable bear the noise any longer and they retreated outside, and on discovering a barn they crawled amongst the hay and continued their sleep in peace.

When awoke the sun was high in the sky; and Berrwynn calculated it was near noon, and again hungry he clutched his coin pouch, then and closely followed by Tresoara they again approached the stone house.

Knocking the door he again received no reply, and finding it was unlocked they warily entered, and in daylight saw it was a long narrow building and containing wooden benches. Inside the entrance door there stood a water trough and at the chamber's far end; and half hidden by a wooden screen, stood a wooden table and on it a plate holding a small amount of bread and beside it in a decorated cup a little wine.

On discovering the food Tresoara gratefully proclaimed "How kind of them to again provide us a meal" but seeing its minuteness Berrwynn scoffing acclaimed was hardly enough to satisfy mouse, but when eaten he politely left a small coin.

From main hall they wandered through a doorway into a smaller room where cloaks with attached hoods hung along its walls, and beyond another doorway leading to the kitchen where they had spent the first part of the previous night.

Seeing leftovers of wise men's morning meal they could not resist the temptation of savouring; and still very hungry continued to eat their fill, and ashamed of their greed Berrwynn had again to leave a larger coin.

Intrigued, they passed through an arched doorway into a larger room containing a row of beds, but as might displease their hosts if were discovered in their private domain, reversed their steps to the outside and where found Gwen their pony in a paddock.

They searched the surrounds for the wise men but still none were to be seen, and having nothing better to do they returned to the riverside, and Berrwynn having become an expert at fishing amused himself catching a few trout.

Thereafter they lay on the riverbank in warm sunshine gazing at the fair location and then noticed that beyond the stone house and half hidden by trees lay a scattering of native dwellings forming a settlement.

Presently, was heard a booming sound; and of which they later discovered was toll of a bell, and curious they made their way to the house and found that the Wise Men had returned and prepared a meal.

Giving them the caught fish, and Berrwynn and Tresoara were invited to share the meal, but no sooner had they sat down than they were again beset by the insufferable Cadfan again trying to convert them to his religion.

Hoping to distract from his annoying zeal Tresoara addressed another wise man on her left side, but unfortunately it was the studious Garmon and who rarely conversed. It was not until another wise man called Dogfan bringing in the meal were able to change the conversation, and having a healthy appetite they enjoyed the roast mutton meal and was followed by cooked apples with honey.

They were surprised to discover that the three wise men were also blood brothers; as their overall resemblances was deceiving, as eldest Cadfan was gaunt and outspoken to even rudeness. Garmon was dour and a little deaf, and if heard when addressed he however was courteous. The youngest brother Dogfan was a rotund cheerful person and his frequent laughter was infectious and which even caused the stern faced Cadfan sometimes to show a glimmer of a smile.

During their evening meal Cadfan concluded that their use of the term 'Wise Men' was inappropriate also vain, and instead they wished be addressed as 'Brother's'. Though stressed they were not all physically related, but otherwise were all Brothers or Sisters in the Lord's service.

In mentioning Sisters they learned there were others, including women who were similarly doing their God's work, though they mainly operated further south and in areas which suffered from serious local hostilities.

As Berrwynn and Tresoara had been fascinated by Davad's mythological tales; they now again enjoyed the Brothers tales relating to characters and of conflicts in their Christian religion.

Similar to bards' tales, Berrwynn found Christian texts had also many anomalies and which equally confused the young couple, such as of one God and which was also three, had no name and he must not be named. Equally confusing was Adam's banishment from Eden for consuming the forbidden fruits, and in contrast was much enjoyed and even encouraged by the pagan gods.

Furthermore, as a warrior Berrwynn could not understand why Romans and who brought the religion to Britain also killed their Lord, and considered lamentable their God did not smite them for their evil deed, as would any respectful pagan god.

The Brothers toiled extra hard to answer Berrwynn's fundamental questions, but both he and Tresoara remained confused, but as not disappoint their hosts and possibly told to leave the sanctuary pretended they understood what were taught.

Aware the young couple were educated and therefore high bred, Cadfan was curious of their origins, and when asked; Berrwynn was reluctant to reveal much of their past in case Blaidd was still searching for them. But as not lie; he merely stated that he was a warrior, and that Tresoara hailed from a mountainous tribe, and though it seemed to satisfy he suspected they had more questions in mind.

Having said were married they were invited to stay and were given the occupancy of a native round hut, and grateful of their hospitality Berrwynn casually thanked them also for the bread and the wine they had provided for their morning meal.

No sooner heard, the Brothers became quiet and searchingly stared at each other, and Cadfan at head of the table slowly arose and his eyes icily glaring he waved his long thin forefinger and angrily expounded. "The Bread you eat, was the flesh of our Lord, and the wine you drank his blood" and with utmost wrath he vehemently declared, "You heathens have eaten our God"

Tresora cowered under his fierce onslaught and fearing a possible horrendous consequence her large brown eyes filled with tears, and finally plucking courage, she; and in a choking voice, innocently asked. "Are we now cannibals"?

Her totally unexpected question again reduced the Brothers into a thoughtful silence, and the usually undemonstrative Garman sitting next to Tresoara sympathetically put his arm around her shoulder. When sufficiently calmed gave her a cloth to wipe away her tears, and possibly forgiving; he made a sign of a cross, blessing her.

Dogfan meanwhile was wary that Cadfan's outburst might arouse the warrir Berrwynn to avenge the distress caused to Tresoara and struggled to find a way of relieving the tension. His only weapon was his sense of humour, and to somehow make light of a considered serious incident he released a tumultuous guffaw of laughter and succeeded in extinguishing the inflammable atmosphere.

Berrwynn was stunned; but not of fear, but astonishment at a ceremony of eating the flesh and drinking blood of their God, and he became convinced he would not join a religion. Of such barbarism; and equalling that of the ancient druidic practises, as condemmed by Romans.

Presumably forgiven, Berrwynn and Tresoara bid the Brothers goodnight and retired to their hut and barring the door they discussed their thoughts of Wise Men and the doubtful religion, and for the first time for days they now enjoyed a long amd uninterrupted sleep.

The following day they wandered into the Avernian native settlement and talked to people and learn of their interpretation of the Brothers and of their religion. The Averians conveyed that since Roman destruction of worship of their goddess Mai their aptitude to religion had remained negative. When the Brothers arrived they at first were suspicious but now had only praise as grateful for improving farming methods and saving them from poverty.

Thereon gladly accepted the benefits and their religion and such as pagan priests, few bards and elders and who were fiercly loyal to the old religion moved out of Maifod, forming a new sttlement on a hill opposite.

The tribesmen informed that disappearances of Brothers during the day time was because were in the fields harvesting crops and tendering to their livestock, and though most the manual work was done by hired men they also often partooke.

It was not until a few days later that they met Golwelan; the seldom seen fourth member or Brother, physically unrelated to the three brothers was very old and cared for by two daughters, the unmarried Myllin and Braid her widowed sister.

White bearded and mournful eyed Golwelan was held in much respect as to his great age and piety.

Berrwynn was surprised to learn that he was privileged born son of a Christian high priest called Manilus of Glasynys, and previously of Caerwen

Born in the east, Manilus had come to Rome to trade in Christian relics, and becoming exceedingly wealthy he was jealously accused of relics' manufacture and unable to prove their authenticity feared persecution. Manilus fled to Gaul, but stories of alleged forged relics preceded his arrival, and continued to Britain.

Amongst many relics Manilus possessed were splinters of wood and nails from the true holy cross which the lord had been crucified and also thorns from the crown of thorns. But his most treasured possession was a drinking vessel, the cup or Holy Chalice the Lord drank from at his last supper.

Possessing such treasures Manilus soon became head priest of the Christian church in the Roman city of Caerwen, but when the pagan Saxons attacked and verging on defeat the hierarchy moved the church's treasures west to Glasynys.

In his old age Manilus appointed his son Golwelan keeper of the holy relics, and behest that he instal in a safe and appropriate shrine and where publicly revered. But it being turbulent times and fearing stolen or destroyed by advancing Saxons he hid the relics in a cave in Mendip Hills, however he became troubled that he had not fulfilled his duty of constructing shrine as to display the relics.

Meeting Golwelan during pilgrimage to Glasynys Cadfan revealed he had created a Christian mission and far enough away from any threat from the pagan Saxons. Golwelan and under the impression his God had arranged the meeting he offered to join him, and as possession of holy relics attracted pilgrims and brought money to his mission Cadfan gladly accepted.

At the new Maifod mission, Golwelan had temporarily stored the relics in a cliff cavity behind the church whilst awaiting construction of a satisfactory shrine and where that they be displayed in all their glory.

Meantime a donation secured whoever ailed to touch and instantly healed, and though non-ailing Berrwynn was curious, and at a price of one of Gardo's gold coins he was privileged the sight of the relics. And though awed the chalice' miraculous healing powers he was a little disappointed when saw the simple ebony wooden cup. However ceded, that its' added gold edgings and inlaid amber geatly enhanced its original simplicity.

Cadfan proudly proclaimed that when the holy relics were duly displayed, Maifod would be the holiest shrine in the land and would attract pilgrims from far and wide.

Berrwynn and Tresoara continued to have their evening meal with the Brothers and as usual Cadfan did most the talking, and revealed he had plans to have further Christian missions and establish a diocese and equalling that of Glasynys.

The mission church's were nearly always deliberately sited on pagan holy places such as stone circles and signifying replacement of the old pagan religion, and inferred Maifod was once an important site of Mai, the goddess of fertility.

Therefore being a pagan name; the Brothers needed a more suitable Christian name for their church, and Garmon suggested "In that it was the Mother Church of a future diocese it be re-named Mair–fod, meaning Mary's abode.

Avernian inhabitants however found Mair'fod difficult to pronounce and despite Brothers' insistence its name prevailed and eventually accepted it remain Maifod.

The young couple were contended to stay in Maifod for the near future and Berrwynn asked the Brothers how he could also assist their community, and latin literate taught the language. Tresoara also integrated with the tribe's women and taught many skills learned from her Roman governesses when in Pendeva.

Several of the converted tribesmen and also women were training to be Christian missionaries and were intend to carry the gospel further a field, and outstanding were two brothers Tysilio and Trinio, also Silyn and Erfil the daughter of Padarn.

The winter was now fast approaching and the weather became extremely wet and caused the river to flood and then was followed by snow, but the loving young couple enjoyed the comforts of a roaring fire in their snug little hut.

Very soon their pagan winter festival would be held and Berrwynn was concerned of the reaction of the Christian Brothers to the pagan festivities. Surprisingly they did not condemn the merrymaking and Dogfan clarified that Christians also enjoyed the festivities as their God was born at this very time.

Native Avernians were Christians, but pagan beliefs die hard and during the midwinter festival mistletoe, ivy, yew and holly branches were hung outside their huts to ward off evil spirits. Pagan festivities were also notorious for drunken revelry and large quantities of intoxicating liquor was consumed whilst they waited until dawn to welcome rebirth, or start of the return of Grian the Sun God.

Though Berrwynn tolerated Christian beliefs but inwardly he was sceptical and was not yet prepared to accept its teachings, but mainly because he feared the wrath of abandoned pagan gods. Tresoara however was receptive of Brothers' persuasions and she approached Dogfan, and he was delighted but relayed that firstly be baptised to receive the Holy Mother's blessing.

Tresoara hoped Berrwynn would also consider converting but when revealed her decision to become Christian he remained uncommitted, but to avoid hurting her feelings he simply advised her submit to her strongest faith. His negative response disappointed Tresoara, however decided to proceed, and subsequently baptised in a font they had previously mistaken for an animal trough.

The end of winter again brought heavy rainstorms and combined with melting snows on the distant mountains the river became immensely swollen and burst its banks and caused much flooding of the valley. And Tresoara was greatly grieved when the Avernwy flood waters swept away and drowned Gwen her loving little pony. This caused Berrwynn concern as whether it was the pagan river goddess' revenge of Tresoara abandoning and becoming a Christian.

When warmer spring weather finally approached, Dogfan and Garmon and whom had families elsewhere welcomed them to Maifod, but Cadfan proclaimed that due to the hard winter their meagre resources could not feed them all.

It was then decided it was time for some of the Brothers to individually travel to new pastures and create the large diocese they previously planned, and newly arrived families as before had regrettably to remain behind until safe to join them.

After the pagan Beltane festival of start of spring, and of which the Christians also celebrated, the Brothers prepared for their new missions. But after massacres of missionaries further south, were extremely nervous of unknown tribesmen of the mountain valleys.

One night as they lay warmly snuggled together in their bed Tresoara unexpectedly announced she was possibly expecting a child, and though Berrwynn had previously contemplated the possibility was momentary shocked, but also extremely joyful.

The happy pair now pondered as whom to approach for their child's blessing, whether Mai the goddess of fertility and birth, or now Tresoara's Christian Holy Mother Mair?

Chapter VI

Missionary Journeys

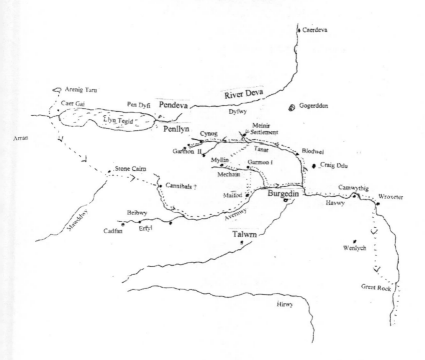

New Missions. Berrwynn becomes protector of Cadfan in Beibwy. Thereafter the Cainwy and Tannwy missions. He meets legionnaire, Emrys of Tannat. Berrwynn arrives in Maenwy. Meets Banhadla Agwyllt, insane priest leader, and kills him.

Berrwynn in needing good care for expectant mother Tresoara was concerned that they had now also to leave Maifod and approaching the Brothers was happily told 'whether stayed or not' was his own choice.

It was assumed Cadfan would remain in Maifod and become leader of the future diocese but he surprised everyone revealing that he was going to establish a new Christian mission in the notoriously dangerous westward Beibwy valley.

Momentary Cadfan was contended for the aged Golwelan the task of Mother Church leader during remainder of his life, and thereafter considered returning.

Besides her young age and inexperience the ever thoughtless Cadfan allowed a young female called Erfyl Llian and to accompany on this dangerous mission.

To accessing the lands adjoining the western sea, a Roman road passed through this valley and protected by numerous small forts, and a long abandoned one was located in lower part of the valley. Called Justin, or natively Einion; and as usual developed into a settlement, and trading with Avernian peoples most its inhabitants were already Christians.

In the narrow valley overlooking the river they had built a church, and knowing no other was also called Mair, and in finding Christianity already established Cadfan immediately continued towards the next settlement up along the valley.

Further up there dwelt real native Beibio tribe's people, and hearing tales of their fierceness the missionaries expected a hostile reception, and regardless of Erfyl's innocence Cadfan was fully intended on persevering.

The intrepid Brother led headlong into what may have been a lion's den, however were surprised to discover that by trading with the previous settlement were also partly influenced, and instead of hostility they were welcomed.

The settlement became their first mission, and on a natural hill above the river they began constructing a little wooden church, and the swift success greatly encouraged them, and earnestly believed their God was now leading them.

Cadfan's dream was not yet complete as he intended reaching the stronghold of the infamous Beibio ap Beibio further up the valley, and such were tales spun of the fearsome tyrant that travellers feared to near tread.

Though Cadfan felt safe in hands of the Lord, he however ceded to others' criticism that he needed someone stronger than Erfyl at his side, and leaving her at the settlement he returned alone to Maifod, bearing news of his initial success.

But declared that to continue into a substantially more hostile environment he needed a stronger advocate by his side, and there was no stronger protector than Berrwynn, and he was most surprised when was asked by Cadfan to protect him.

Berrwynn however was not entirely convinced Cadfan needed him as already had the protection of his God. Furthermore pagan, and Berrwynn's first reaction was to immediately decline as he considered was more his duty to be with his pregnant young wife.

Baptised into the Christian faith, Tresoara however encouraged him to go, and stated it was a long time until birth of the baby, and against his better judgment, but not wanting to disappoint his loving young wife Berrwynn reluctantly agreed.

It was a sad day; when and for the first time since their marriage parted with Tresoara, and soon he and Cadfan and another newly arrived young missionary called Tydecho crossed Avernwy river and entered the Beibwy river valley.

They anxiously hurried to Erfyl at the middle settlement, and when again met were very relieved was unharmed, and in contrast she happily relayed the tribesmen had given their full support in establishing the mission church.

Viewing, they were surprised at the progress of its construction, but Cadfan was impatient to continue and their stay at the middle settlement mission was short.

Leaving Erfyl at her now mission, the next day Cadfan, Berrwynn and their Avernian helpers with their pack-laden mules arrived at the heart of the much feared main settlement of Garth-Beibio.

In meeting the infamous Beibio ap Beibio they found him merry through drink and momentary friendly, and much to Berrwynn's exasperation the outspoken Cadfan precipitously announced he had come to make them all Christians.

Berrwynn tried to restrain him, but was to no avail and impetuously continued, and declaring that he would allow no heathen priest to stand in his way'.

Hearing his bold pronouncement Beibio tribes' people were utterly shocked and nervously glanced at their leader expecting a tirade, but uncharacteristically; he and instead of ordering their instant deaths, oppositely roared with laughter.

Berrwynn and exceptionally relieved was surprised were not harmed, and debated as whether it was Cadfan's sheer boldness; or as the missionaries believed; their Unnamed God had secured their deliverance.

Cadfan callously assumed that Beibio's fearsome reputation was wildly exaggerated and purely based on his forebears' refusal to bow to the Romans.

Berrwyn was however sceptical of his naïve presumptions and specified that Beibio was presently merrily intoxicated, but when sober no one could anticipate his unpredictable nature.

Beibio was exceptionally fond of feasting and merrymaking and invited them into his dwelling for a feast and where large quantities of intoxicating liqueur was freely available, and the more he indulged, the friendlier he became.

Unbelievably, it seemed their mission had proved effective as the great Beibio in between imbibing questioned them about their mission, and it seemed he was possibly interested in the teachings.

Towards end of the evening the missionaries were again surprised when the much inebriated Beibio announced that he personally would build a house to their God. And with same breath he ordered his pagan head priest to also be a Christian and to obey teachings their new; and Christian priest.

The displaced pagan priest became furiously angry in losing his long held power, and threatened fire and damnation on the missionaries, but Cadfan's unmoveable faith in the will of the Unnamed God and he dismissed the pagan priest's threats.

Thereafter and thoroughly intoxicated with his most magnificent triumph Cadfan happily retired to his allocated hut for the night.

Berrwynn was also pleased the mission had been successful, and as Cadfan secured entirely on his own merit he judged he was also capable of securing his own safety. And very anxious of Tresoara he decided to return early on the morrow.

Suffering consequences of the previous day's indulgences Beibio was the next day in no mood to listen to the pagan priest's protestations and ordered his head removed from his body, and thereafter he happily retired to his bed for the day.

When learned of the priest's violent death Cadfan was horrified and he frantically searched for Berrwynn, and to his dismay found that he; and ignorant of eventual consequences, had departed for Maifod very early in the morning.

It was not until later did Cadfan learn that Beibio intensely disliked the pagan priest; and as not for probable wrath of pagan gods he would have had him killed long ago, and having now a more powerful God he safely rid of him.

Berrwynn happily proceeded eastwards and in course of his journey came across a hunter; and coincidentally the same he had met the previous year, and in their conversation the hunter disclosed that he also came from Burgedin.

The hunter had not until now recognized Berrwynn and declared that Burgedin people assumed that after their elopement he and Tresoara had safely escaped to Caerdeva or possibly in Brigantia Manceinion.

He also relayed that Rhiannon was well but as ever was anxious for his safety, and further revealed that Anwar; and now aged, greatly suffered from the after-effects of his war wounds. Blaidd of Carrog; was still alive but he suffered from severe paralysis and could no longer walk, and Braan his eldest son was now tribe leader.

Berrwynn was extremely pleased with news of his family and he asked the hunter to convey a message to his mother; promising to visit when Christian Brothers no longer needed his services. However he was very careful to reveal only what wished Rhiannon to presently know and omitted mentioning the expected offspring; as knew that at the earliest opportunity she would seek her first grandchild.

Paying the hunter a coin for his trouble Berrwynn then continued on his journey.

The Second Mission

Arriving back in Maifod Berrwynn found Tresoara well and extremely pleased to see him, but discovered Dogfan and Garmon impatiently awaiting his return, and barely arrived he was also asked to protect their intended mission.

He however had no intention of again leaving Tresoara until birth of their child, but during his absence Tresoara promised the Brothers she would not prevent and encourage him to accompany them.

Berrwynn was torn between what considered wisest, or otherwise please his dear wife and however unwise, and exasperated he consulted Golwelan; who had lost his first wife in pregnancy. When asked his opinion as whether he thought that he should stay and care his pregnant wife Golwelan was strangely uncommitted, and replied; if decided to leave, his daughter Braid would nurse Tresoara.

Against his better judgement Berrwynn finally ceded to Tresoara's extraordinary wish, but insisted was postponed for the few more precious days that he wished to be together, and plans which best suited him were made for oncoming journey.

This northern mission party consisted of Garmon, Dogfan and his three sons, Cynog, Illog and younger son also called Garmon, and controversially Myllin the elder daughter of Golwelan.

Berrwynn tried to dissuade Myllin, but staunchly she resisted his attempts of her exclusion, eventually and in being of masculine physique was disguised in male garb. Golwelan's other daughter Braid remained in Maifod to care for her aged father and also tasked of nursing Tresoara, and two local convert brothers Tysilio and Trinio also stayed and administered the missionary's families left behind.

The day of departure came far too soon, and they gathered together outside the Maifod settlement and bid farewell, and the party soon passed over woody hill pass and into the fertile Cainwy valley.

The valley was famed for abundance of wild boars and much hunted by adventurous young Romans from Virconium, and combined their boar hunts callously raping the native maidens. Thereafter the tribes' people became extremely reluctant to reveal their presence to any strangers.

Reaching the Cainwy valley the missionaries found it was as they had expected woody fertile and noticeably their lands was tilled and livestock grazed and all was peaceful.

Descending towards the riverside they discovered a small settlement consisting of about five round huts, nearby children happily played in the river, and in arriving introduced themselves to the tribesmen. They found these people were friendly but a trifle reserved and seemed anxious but they volunteered no explanations.

Invited to sit down to meal and afterwards they congratulated their hosts on their hospitality, and Garmon rewarded their dignitaries with silver bangles; and which he had engraved Christian emblems.

Berrwynn was amazed at the missionary's' clever technique, designing objects to arouse curiosity and of which hopefully would lead to some religious discussions. Afterwards they sat around the fire talking, and not necessary of religion but also of general topics such as of farming and tribal relations, and mention of the latter brought a silent response.

Getting dark; they were given a hut to sleep, and after their tiring journey spent a comfortable night sleep but very early the following morning were awakened by the sounds of many feet entering the settlement. On later questioning about the commotion, one of them declared they had been on patrols in hills bordering the next valley, and two warriors had been hurt in a minor scuffle.

Dogfan; and who could practically turn his hand to handling of any profession, cook, entertainer, and also a physician, and after examining the two victims he administered some medical aid and bounded their injured limbs with cloth.

It was then they were informed that the tribe was at war with the Tannat valley people and since the days of their forefathers; and was believed it started by the kidnapping of a maid from the tribe by a son of their local leader.

When Berrwynn heard the tale he was astounded as to its similarity to his own, but fortunately his amorous exploit had not developed into a tribal war, but he chillingly realised that it could very easily have resulted in the spilling of blood.

This conflict was even sadder; as most the inhabitants of the two valleys were of the same blood, descendants of Cornovii tribe and who alike Burgedin factor had dispersed into these woody adjoining valleys.

In further discussions the missionaries learned the Cainwy people dearly wished for peace but knew not how to achieve, as the Tannat valley enemies were led by a self installed and unapproachable fanatical priest called Banhadla Agwyllt.

This news was grave for Dogfan; as this northernmost Tannat valley had been his designated mission, and now they could not risk a frontal approach over the mountain; as in coming from enemy's valley they would be regarded as hostile.

It seemed a difficult proposition of how to approach the valley, and Berrwynn's military experience offered the solution, proposed that they approach the valley from a neutral direction.

Berrwynn briefly knew the Tannat river valley, as it was through its untamed wilderness of thick woods and marshes the Burgedin and Carrog tribes' people travelled to other's lands. However, he knew very little of the valley's inhabitants as on the long journeys he rarely saw its peoples, and personally assumed that the valley was practically uninhabited.

THE TANNAT MISSION

Dogfan was still keen to continue the mission but rested in the settlement in the Cainwy valley for a few weeks and during that time revealed nothing of future plans to the tribes' people until their imminent departure.

Garmon the Elder decided to stay in reverently peaceful Cainwy, and because of tales of the ferocity of the fanatical priest Banhadla Agwyllt, Berrwynn insisted that Myllin also stay behind in Cainwy.

Thereafter Dogfan, his three sons Cynog, Illog and Garmon the Younger and with Berrwynn leading firstly proceeded eastwards downstream following Cain River to its confluence with the sparklingly clean Tannat tributary.

Whilst sat eating their provisions on the river bank Berrwynn contemplated what would be the Tannat people's reaction to their intrusion, as all they possessed to defend themselves was his own short sword and hidden dagger. Though anxious of the dangers they may face, such were the Brothers' faith in their God; carried nothing except their rood wooden crosses.

Personally Berrwynn had doubts as to the wisdom of challenging their native gods and also felt guilty persuading the people to change religion and a way of life enjoyed since ancient times. But he revealed not his feelings to the Brothers as he knew it would be useless, as their faith in the righteousness of their cause was unshakeable.

Resuming the journey up the Tannat River and in a while they came across an inhabitant and expecting a hostile reception they were much surprised when he cheerfully greeted. The stranger seemed to have no inhibitions of the fact that he must have known they had come from Cainwy, and by his speech and fine clothes Berrwynn recognised that he was no mere native; but a Romano/Celt nobleman.

The stranger announced his name was Ambrosius Fluvius, a British born Roman and originally from Virconium; and sensing possible hostility hurriedly added that he was natively called Emrys. In following conversations he informed that on leaving the legions he had built a villa at near his wife's birthplace in this valley, and learning they were Christians he proudly proclaimed that he had established a church in nearby settlement.

Dogfan was agast in hearing that Christianity was already established, and that he had been preceded and was stolen what he considered was to be his destiny, thwarting his long ambition to establish a church and bearing his own name.

Inner soul searching, Dogfan concluded that the Unnamed God was possibly punishing him for this vanity, and vowed if he ever established a church it would never bear his own name. After offering his painful penance assumed forgiven, and which comfortably relieved his feelings, and thereafter wondered as whether the Lord had even greater tasks for him to perform.

The missionaries were led to a little church officiated by its priest Blodwel located in a delightful little dell by the riverside and when Dogfan saw that the settlement only comprised of two huts he turned away and wryly smiled.

Afterwards they were invited to Emrys' villa located two miles away, and during their meal they questioned as whether Tannat valley tribesmen were as fiercely hostile as had been led to believe by Cainwy people.

Blodwel had been Emrys' Saxon slave, and released by him was forever grateful and remained his extremely servile long time servant, and appreciating his loyalty Emrys granted him priesthood of the church.

Blodwel however was dissuasive of them continuing their mission, and warned that three miles away lay a mountain top fort manned by pagan warriors who guarded the pass to Cainwy. But hearing his pessimistic declaration Emrys assured they need not fear the guarding warriors, as their sole object was in defending the pass and would be unconcerned of a small passing party.

Berrwynn suspiciously assumed that Blodwel was jealously guarding his future priestly diocese when further warned that upstream lay the utmost danger from the priest-chief Banhadla Agwyllt, and who had no restrain in taking of lives.

He revealed that Orog; their long time leader and who caused the conflict against Cainwy, had been challenged and finally ousted by Banhadla by him promising to end the conflict, but he became an even worst tyrannical leader.

With seemingly utmost sincerity he further proclaimed it was sheer madness for such small party; and without protection of a strong military escort, to approach this evil and insane monster. Suspecting he was lying or least was exaggerating because objected to the missionaries' trespassing on what he regarded his own, however Berrwynn as missionaries' protector was obliged to reveal the sobering accounts.

When asked whether they wished to continue, and firmly embedded in their faith and also in Berrwynn, the missionaries unanimously opted to proceed on their missionary westwards march.

As the party neared the foot of a steep conical shaped hill they could see on its summit earth battlements and smoke arising from unseen huts behind them, and undisturbed they quietly continued their journey. For the next few miles they travelled; and possibly unseen, and through a beautiful valley surrounded by oak covered hills, and they reached a fast flowing tributary when night was falling.

They now decided to rest for the night and in looking for a suitable place to camp they followed the tributary brook upstream, and within a narrow side valley they unexpectedly came across a large settlement.

Berrwynn now realised why; when travelled through the valley he hardly ever saw the inhabitants, as invariably the tribes' people lived in side-valleys and hidden from passing Roman soldiers.

A little fearful of what Blodwel had proclaimed, Berrwynn's small missionary party approached the settlement with caution, and without the forthright Cadfan; Berrwynn; and a pagan, became the spokesman of the Christians missionaries.

Entering the settlement found consisted of more than fifteen round huts and encountered three tall standing stones and which they puzzled as to their purpose. Berrwynn however secretly mused. 'Surely sacrificial stones and where victims are tied and publicly executed, but kept his thoughts to himself.

Soon they were confronted by some tribes' people, and Berrwynn announced to a young man whom seemed to be prominent, that they had come in peace, and seeing were of no threat the tribesmen appeared friendly.

On enquiring, the tribesmen declared they were mostly of the original Maengwyn tribe, and a young man he assumed leader dragged Berrwynn aside and covertly revealed that they were miserably locked in a fruitless war with Cainwy. Resulting in tragic loss of lives and draining their food resources and their children were dying of hunger. He then warned "Beware of our leader the priest Banhadla, and who holds power by terrifying the people with horrendous ceremonial sacrifices to Meinir the goddess of the Maenwy River".

Continuing, he relayed "Maenwy is this tributary river which flows from its source in distant peaks and continues over a great cliff into a water-carved bowl at its base before continues its journey down the valley. The goddess Meinir desired children but an unnamed god of above peak had no wish to associate with the evil goddess; and therefore lacked offspring".

Reducing his voice to a whisper, he revealed the horrific sacrificial practices as instigated by their priest. "In his madness of trying to achieve acceptability of the childless Meinir, Banhadla every year forcefully takes a babe from its mother and presents to the goddess at the festival of fertility. The ceremony includes taking the seized infant onto the height of the waterfall, and on rising of the sun on first morning of Beltane ceremoniously drops the babe from waterfall's great height.

If falls into the water carved bowl at the base of the waterfall it figuratively has entered the womb of Meinir, however as yet; not a one babe has achieved the bowl, and every year shattered on the rocks below.

Berrwynn was absolutely shocked at the revelations, and so horrendous he found hard to believe, but precautionary took Dogfan aside and disclosed what he had been told. The Christian Brother was also shocked at the alleged tale of extreme cruelty; but as the Unnamed God had sent them here on a mission and were adamant to continue despite the possible dire consequences.

After spending the night in an empty dwelling the missionaries early the next morning were confronted by the extremely agitated high priest Banhadla; and who they found was a hideously ugly and much tattooed giant of a man.

Being a physician Dogfan immediately recognised Banhadla's very dangerous psychotic condition and was not a difficult diagnosis as Berrwynn recognised that when aroused could be extremely dangerous, and momentary was wildly aroused.

Without introducing himself Banhadla directly accused them of being spies, and despite their denials he ordered associate priests to seize Dogfan's three sons and tie them to the stone pillars.

The Christian missionary party's fate now lay in the hands of the insane Banhadla and his servile priests' and Berrwynn realised there was very little they could do to defend themselves against them, and also probably against their whole tribe.

He now regretted getting involved in the Brothers' missions, and having to face death on Christian behalf and whilst was still pagan, and same as the tribesmen.

Recalling the young man who the previous day had whispered his resentment of the evil priest; he contemplated that in their discontentment there was possibly a faint glimmer of hope. Clutching at straws Berrwynn now to gambled on the assumption that a number of the regime's opponents were assembled in the square, and if he killed Banhadla they might possibly be unafraid to take control.

When the raging tattooed giant bent his head forward to speak directly to smaller built Dogfan standing at Berrwynn's side; and resolving not to show any sign of weakness, he grasped the opportune moment.

Slowly he extracted his dagger from its scabbard; and as if he was drawing the bow across a fiddle, meticulously drew its sharp serrated edge down the side of Banhadla's thick neck.

Nearly severing his ugly head from his large body the square gathered crowd gasped at his bold a deed and in petrified silence watched priest's blood spurt like a fountain from the gaping wound, and splattering all within reach.

However; it was not all yet over, and Berrwynn slowly advanced and protectively stood alone ahead of members of the missionary party anxiously waiting for the reaction of other priests. Possibly also the crowd; as he was still unsure if had their support, and though gallantry faced the priests he had no illusions of defeating the whole tribe.

But if to be massacred, his pagan instincts prevailed that firstly he extract a painful vengeance, and when subordinate priests overcame their initial shock and now with their faces showing their intense outrage, advanced with daggers drawn.

Still holding the blood soaked dagger Berrwynn extracted his sword, and holding the dagger in his left hand and sword in the other he bravely faced them alone, and forwardly thrusting his sword he instantly killed the first priest. Then with his dagger he tore open the second priests' fat belly and spilled out his over ample intestines and he fell to the ground fatally wounded.

His senses sharpened in his singular engagement; Berrwynn at first failed to hear the shouting of surrounding crowds of tribesmen, and realising that they were screaming "kill, kill, kill", he assumed this was his and missionaries' end.

Brandishing knives; and led by the young man whom had spoken the previous day, the tribesmen surged forward and much to the relief of terrified Brother's and also Berrwynn they instead proceeded to hack the remaining priests to death.

Banhadla and four priests were now dead but the fifth priest managed to escape, and seeing was over the crowd triumphantly and unceremoniously seized the corpses and threw into the river, and they were swept away in the fast current.

A young man was heard say, "Banhadla, you have now achieved what most desired, as now and forever you are joined with Meinir the evil river goddess".

Untying Illog, Cynog and Garmon and were warmly embraced, and the young man and whose name they discovered was Evor warmly thanked Berrwynn saying. "You have released us from our suffering of many years we have endured under the insane sacrificial priest, and now dead and so also shall his evil cult".

It seemed possible to the missionaries that Maenwy people would now adopt the Christian religion, and to further gain their confidence Dogfan firstly took on the roll of a physician of attending to the sick and wounded.

Once again Berrwynn was amazed at the Brothers triumph, and with aid of their Unnamed God had swept away all their enemies before them, and he now also became to believe in their God and intended to accept when returned to Maifod.

The inhabitants came together to discuss the matter of ending the fruitless war which decimated the population, but firstly they needed a new leader they could trust and asked for Berrwynn. But he declined their offer saying he had soon to return to Maifod, and proposed that the young man Evor whom had bravely long opposed Banhadla Agwyllt's harsh regime.

Evor and without much opposition was selected leader of the tribe, and the people impressed by their salvation from the evil priests through the action of Unnamed God declared they could build their mission church in Maenwy.

Dogfan was delighted when many clamoured to be baptised, but he declined Maenwy river water as to its association with the evil goddess, searching the mountains for a spiritually uncontaminated source. When eventually found a suitable spring were baptised, and thereafter the spring became known as Dogfan's Well.

In the weeks that followed the church was completed, and tribesmen wished it be called after Dogfan, but he having experienced near death and saved by the mercy of his God and declined their offer. Declaring his God required him to be also humble remained unnamed, and because of the goddess also the settlement and simply referred to as 'Enclosure or Settlement on the rapid flowing brook'.

However, many years later the church was dedicated to Dogfan and though his baptismal springs hallowed his name, was not included in name of the settlement.

Needing to include the tribesmen in ceremonial display they were encouraged to convert the stone sacrificial pillars into Christian crosses by fastening crossed wood stake with cords at nearly their top. One cross was to remain in the square, another at the church, and plans were made for the remaining cross to be placed on summit of the pass leading to the Cainwy valley; as their sign of peace.

Eventually the crossed pillar was dragged by oxen to the summit and erected and facing Cainwy valley: informing their enemies that were now Christians, and now that their leader Banhadla's tyranny was over they wished to end the long war.

The peace symbol was successful and blood related enemies warily approached each other, the leaders shook each other's hands as embracing was out of the question as the both sides had lost many kinfolk, and only passage of time could entirely heal the great wounds.

Thereafter the hill pass was named *Bwlch y Ddor* or 'Pass of the (Open) Door', as was to be their doorway to renewed peace, hope and of friendship.

Chapter VII

A Further Mission

Berrwynn's westwards journey, establishing further missions. The Sanctuary Valley. Berrwynn returns to Tresoara in Maifod. – Faces his utmost Tragedy.

At last Berrwynn thought his missionary work had ended and joyfully looked forward to again see his dearest Tresoara and possibly also an arrived child.

The young missionaries Cynog, Illog and Garmon the younger, however revealed that they also intended establishing missions; and in the upper reaches of the Tannat river valley.

Since elimination of Banhadla Agwyllt they assumed they no longer needed Berrwynn's protection, but Dogfan busily establishing his church was concerned that they were too inexperienced to deal with hostilities they may possibly encounter. They were now going to the unpredictable old leader Orog's, territory, and Dogfan pleaded Berrwynn accompany them, but having faithfully served and nearly lost his life on their behalf was dismayed when again asked.

But having become a good friend of Dogfan placed him in a dilemma; as he would be unable to forgive himself if harmed, and again reluctantly agreed to accompany the brothers. But most strongly impressed it was only on the premise that as soon confirmed his sons were in no danger he would immediately return, and continue on to Maifod.

A few days later Berrwynn and the three young brothers and five local tribesmen left Maenwy settlement and headed westwards up the valley and they soon arrived at where another valley departed south westerly.

Illog insisted that he and three protective tribesmen access the smaller valley and the remainder and under Berrwynn continued west along the main Tannat River.

Berrwynn having passed this way before, and at each encounter he never failed to amaze when confronted the immense rocky mountainside arising in innumerable cliffs from the flat and marshy valley floor. The accompanied tribesmen declared that atop the mountain lay the fort and it was where Orog after been toppled by Banhadla safely resided, but they knew not whether he still inhabited.

Below the towering mountain the valley widened and after a difficult crossing of a marsh arrived at where divided into another two distinct valleys, and on a high ground perfectly dividing the valleys they came across a remains of a stone circle. Nearby there were a few ramshackle round huts and their occupiers were very much akin the hungry looking inhabitants Berrwynn previously encountered in Pen Avernwy and of whom Tresoara assumed cannibalistic.

When greeted, they suspiciously replied in their ancient tongue, and Berrwynn conversant of their language heard them anxiously enquiring of their accompanied Maenwy tribesmen, "Who are these strangers?"

They replied, were Christians, and meant them no harm, and reassuringly further informed their presence would much enhance their lives, as Christians could dispense magic and which they called miracles.

Hopelessly misconstruing Christian teachings, they also and disastrously stated they could turn stones into bread and water to wine, and they had once fed five thousand people with only five bread loaves and two trout.

The tribesmen firmly believed in magic as dispensed by wizards or pagan priests, but never before had deities offered food and of any kind, and which was a very scarce commodity in these over hunted high valleys.

Such great magic intrigued the hungry inhabitants, and as the Christian's God was surely the most bountiful he was surely the one they also needed the most.

Missionaries' fame spread, and many; including hilltop fort's occupiers flocked to see and hopefully sample these ever wonderful gifts.

Excitedly, anticipated that their rock-strewn mountainsides turned into scarcely acquired bread and the clear but tasteless water into delicious wine, a commodity only Romans afforded and of which they also had long wished to taste.

Cynog, the eldest brother was very angry when he learned their mission had been misinterpreted, and declared that he could not perform miracles or of even simple illusory tricks. The situation became near facetious as he had now to ask the pagan Berrwynn's advice of how could maintain the tribesmen's trust in Christianity when became known that they could do no magic or miracles.

They feared that when discovered there was no free bread or any covetous wine they would believe that they had been deceived and lead to volatile reaction, and Berrwynn was also perplexed, and he even asked his pagan gods for guidance.

Receiving no miraculous answer he had now alone find a subtle way of admitting to the tribesmen that the missionaries had nothing more to offer than their Christian teachings.

With Cynog by his side, Berrwynn perilously began, hoping that he somehow could convey to the would-be feasting participant tribesmen that they had been mistakenly informed. But no sooner revealed Christians had no magical formulae to turn the stones into bread or their water into wine it turned into a noisy frenzy and followed by a hail of stones. Witnessing drawn knives it was apparent the missionaries were now in mortal danger and in fear of their lives they swiftly withdrew and barricaded themselves inside a native hut.

As the commotion outside increased they prayed to the Christian God for rescue from the baying mob, but Berrwynn was sceptical would answer, but pledged that if Unnamed God came to their aid, he would also believe and become a Christian.

Their salvation however did not directly come from where they expected, but from Orog whom having miserably occupied the hilltop fort since displaced by Banhadla and learning of his adversary's fate he was now immensely grateful.

Orog came down from his fortress and stood between enraged tribesmen and the missionaries cowering in the hut, and when calmed the atmosphere he called the missionaries to emerge.

Berrwynn; but within the comparative safety of protective doorway, professed an apology on the missionaries' behalf, and seemingly tribesmen still feared Orog as surprisingly they accepted it had been a regrettable misunderstanding.

The old leader instructed the tribesmen to repeat after him a binding oath. "In that despite not filling our bellies with miracle bread or fulfilling dreams of permanent intoxication, we are eternally grateful to Christians for ridding of Banhadla".

Whether wily Orog's intervention was motivated to curry Berrwynn favours, hoping he would assist him regaining leadership, and though grateful of saving their lives Berrwynn however resolved not take sides in their local politics.

The missionaries sighed in relief at somewhat resolved outcome, and though their attempt at converting the tribesmen to Christianity was not wholly satisfactory however they were allowed to build a church.

Constructed within the abandoned stone circle with nearby ample scatterings of the very stones which their people previously expected be turned to bread, and the irony was not missed by Cynog. In his first sermon professed that the stones of the church were now their holy bread, and rain which leaked through its reed roof their wine, and symbolically the church was the body and blood of the Lord.

According to number of appearances of the moon Tresora was near delivery of their child and at last putting his own and also his family's need before Brothers' Berrwynn was determined to immediately return to Maifod.

The tribesmen had spoken of another settlement and the youngest brother Garmon and the only one without a mission was overjoyed that there was another and untouched settlement. But Berrwynn in having many times travelled through the valley denied of its existence, but Garmon insisted that the valley to their left travelled for further three miles and at its end another settlement.

Furthermore it contained a mysterious sect whom claimed were 'Keepers of the Heavenly Chariot' and to Berrwynn's utmost exasperation he announced that he was going to establish his own mission there.

When made enquiries local tribe's people said it was correct, but warned that access to the valley was forbidden unless approved by their goddess; however if she was disobeyed her wrath was unmerciful.

As tribesmen were afraid to venture Berrwynn also forbid Garmon to alone go up the unknown valley, and thinking he had rejoined Cynog Berrwynn started on his own return journey back to Maifod.

Bypassing Cynog's mission, and then also Maenwy he searched for the hill pass to the Caenwy settlement, and before long crossed into the Cain valley, and only realised there were two passes when had not seen their newly erected cross.

Inadvertently, he had entered an unknown large settlement and was surprised to discover it had also a church and enquiring he surprisingly discovered that it was established by Myllin; the strong-hearted daughter of Golwelan.

After they had initially left Cainwy settlement tribesmen had revealed presence of this larger settlement and Myllin aggrieved at being abandoned was determined to surpass the men, venturing west she found a positive response to her teachings.

Berrwynn had now to swallow his pride and admit had not acknowledging her strong personality, and acutely sensitive of male domination Myllin was elated.

Early the next morning Berrwynn joyously left the mission and headed towards the woody hill pass which led to Avernwy valley and eventually Maifod where his dearest; and with very possibly now a child would be waiting for him.

Berrwynn now felt enhanced by presence of an unknown deity, but knew not who guided him, and thinking of Tresoara he became convinced it was Mother Mair.

When emerged from the wood shadowed pass into Avernwy valley he enjoyed glorious morning sunshine on his face, and believed Mother Mair was welcoming him, and the sun's warmth was her approved blessings.

As he hurriedly made his way towards Maifod; a young man tilling a field and seeing Berrwynn he dropped his plough and ran towards the church, and before Berrwynn reached Golwelan came out the door and approached him.

When neared, Berrwynn noticed he had more than the usual mournful face, and looking sadly at him Golwelan and choked with emotion spurted out "She has died" and slowly repeated "Tresoara has died in childbirth, and also the child".

Stunned, Berrwynn could not believe what he heard, and hoping he had possibly misheard; asked Golwelan to repeat, but the old priest; and nearly speechless, was only able to briefly repeat "Tresoara is dead". He then turned and slowly walked with his head bowed towards the church, entering he closed the door behind him and all became deathly silent.

It took quite a while for Berrwynn to able asses the tragic news, and when did, his whole body became numb and he devastatingly sank helpless onto his knees in the newly ploughed earth. Feeling the heat of midday sun on his back he reflected that only hours earlier had thought it was Mother Mair's expressing her blessing. But the hot rays were now burning the back of his exposed neck and it seemed instead it was unforgiving pagan gods extracting their long held revenge.

Oblivious of time he stayed motionless in the muddy field and only sound he heard was river water gushing over the stepping stones at the ford, and it seemed like a whispering female voice saying "Come in to me; and again meet Tresoara".

Seriously considering the seductive proposal; Berrwynn was saved from suicide when realised Tresoara had been baptised a Christian and therefore she would not be alongside a pagan river goddess.

He then arose and unsteadily walked towards the church and when reached he spotted a heap of fresh brown earth covered with bunches of withered flowers and he immediately knew it was Tresoara's grave.

Golwelan; who been watching, reappeared at the door and confirmed its presence, and he invited Berrwynn in for a meal and bed for the night, and leaving him alone at the graveside returned inside.

Kneeling by the graveside Berrwyn felt much alone, and his thoughts turned to what now seemed a long time ago; but it was only the previous day when he had planned his own acceptance of the Christian faith. He no longer wished to convert to the Christian religion, and therefore thought was inappropriate for him to accept Golwelan's invitation to enter the church for a meal and a night's lodging.

A while later Berrwynn heard a sharp bark and his ear was ferociously licked by Tresoara's little bitch dog Dwyn, and more than anything it was her affectionate greeting which most lifted his sad heart. Taking her in his arms he held her tightly to his chest, and as he would have greeted his dearest Tresoara.

He stayed at the graveside a long while wondering what he should now do and eventually came to a decision that he would go a long way away and perhaps rejoin his uncle Taran fighting the Saxons. On the same lines; he considered that if suffered an honourable death in battle he would thus enter Nevol, and a paradise Christians also say enter, and hopefully be again be with his Tresoara.

Having arrived at a positive decision it somewhat invigorated him and getting to his feet he gently placed a white quartz stone at head of grave, then whispered "Sleep well my dearest Tresoara, until we meet again"

With a last look at the grave Berrwynn sadly walked away towards the river and with Dwyn racing away ahead, but at the riverbank the little bitch failed to stop and tumbled into the dark waters. Unable to fight the strong current was swept away and Berrwynn plunged into the river calling its name, fortunately he was able to save; and further tragedy was prevented.

Distraught and in raging anger Berrwynn cried out, "Averna, you and the most heartless of goddesses, what limit to your vengeance? You have taken my dearest Tresoara and our child. Previously Gwen her pony and you now also attempt to take her dear little dog Dwyn, and my last and only remaining link with my Tresoara"?

CHAPTER VIII

BERRWYNN REJOINS TARRAN

Averna visits Berrwynn in a dream. He visits Rhiannon in Burgedin. Continues his journey, meets Ebron. Corinium and meets Tarran. Saxon battles, Tarran dies. Message from Rhianno, he returns. Meets' Silures. Brychan entertains. Thereafter meets Llyr. Berrwynn finally arrives back in Burgedin.

Strenuously, and throughout a long night Berrwynn followed the Avernwy River downstream and near daybreak exhaustively collapsed amongst saplings lining the river bank, and pulling his fleece snugly around himself he fell fast asleep.

From afar he visualised a matronly figure approaching and at first thought it was his mother, but when neared perceived it was a stranger. Reaching him she knelt by his side, and in stooping her sumptuous wavy brown hair reminiscent of a flowing river fell over her face. And in her closeness Berrwynn smelled aroma of wet river moss and young alder leaves.

In a soft melodious voice reassuringly spoke "Be not afraid, I am Averna, your' loving patron since you and Tresoara first came within my sphere, also the bright star at your head at night and feet at dawn; and is testimony of my guardianship.

My visitation is to rectify your erroneous belief that it was by my ordinance that your dearest Tresoara and child have died, and hereby come to assure you it was long ordained, and therefore irreversible, and soon you will learn reason why."

Having delivered her message; Averna bent down and kissed Berrwynn's face, and the moment her lips touched his cheek he awoke, and touching the tickling moisture he found that it was Dwyn licking his face.

For a long time Berrwynn lay reflecting the dream or possibly an apparition and which revealed Averna kind and gentle goddess, totally opposite of what he had previously assumed, and was now much ashamed.

Needing someone to blame he vented his anger at the Christian Brothers for persuading Tresoara to encourage him to protect them at near time birth of their first offspring.

The image of Averna brought him memories of his mother, and when reached the river's confluence Berrwynn wearily sat on the bank thinking of her and other members of his family in Burgedin. And still very tired; he lay back in the warm morning sun and succumbed to overwhelming desire to sleep, and he slept for some hours until he was abruptly aroused by noises of a hunting party.

The huntsmen; and from Burgedin, immediately recognised Berrwynn, and they asked him to accompany them back to the settlement, and in dire need of friendly company, he was easily persuaded.

Lent a fast horse, he galloped ahead to meet his mother and siblings, and entering Burgedin he was delighted to be so welcomed, and was obviouse they held no misgivings of his past misconduct. Rebuffing tribal leadership and for his own selfish enjoyment, and eloping with Blaidd's daughter and irrespective of his mother's choice of Marchell as his wife.

Having not seen his mother since his departure to Pendeva over four years earlier and when they again met both were overjoyed, and seeing he was unaccompanied Rhiannon naturally asked of Tresoara. But when tried to explain that she had died he became distressed; and for the first time since the tragedy released his tied emotions and woefully wept on his mother's shoulder.

When heard the sad news through his emotionally choked voice Rhiannon could do very little to comfort, and she also became distressed and cried tears of pity for her loving son's loss of Tresoara and for her first grandchild she never saw.

The loveable attention of his mother, family and the friendliness of fellow tribe's people immensely assisted Berrwynn in becoming adjusted to his great loss, and seemed he was regaining his past vigour and enthusiasm.

Rhiannon perceived that Berrwynn was now of changed character from when had departed for Pendeva, proudly recognised that he was now a strong fully matured and responsible person, and apparently capable of taking on his leadership roll.

Berrwynn's exterior appearances however shrouded his immense grief of loss of Tresoara, and when Rhiannon enquired of his delayed leadership intentions she was shocked and hurt when again declined.

He revealed that he was soon leaving to join Tarran in the Saxon southern wars, and Rhiannon; who did not naturally plead, earnestly asked him not be so hasty to leave Burgedin. Adding "Antwyn is now old and often unwell, and I also am aging and would struggle to rule alone, and if your stepfather dies in your absent I fear that your brothers Geraint and Llewelyn may quarrel as whom be the leader".

Besides Rhiannon's sound reasons for him remaining, Berrwynn steadfastly intended otherwise, obsessively felt an unknown force was compelling him to continue his plan. When the time came to part; Berrwynn left Dwyn in Rhiannon's care, and after bidding her and tearful family farewell, and without a backward glance as not show his own near tears, he headed downstream.

Bypassing Camwy he duly arrived in Virconium and acquired lodgings for the night, the next day he toured the town searching for armaments and a trusty war horse. Conversing in a meal house he discovered that a battalion of recruits had left for the south the previous day, and as the carts were heavily laden with arms were slow moving. He was further informed he would sooner make contact if he avoided the river's wide curve and instead travel directly south to northern ford of the Severn at a Great Rock.

He was also warned of a fearsome Aryan race called Angles and rumoured to be advancing westwards, and on him enquiring who were the Angles, they replied no one surely knew. Some declared were long established by Romans' vacated Icene lands after their subsequent massacre, but others said only recently invaded from across the sea. Berrwynn concluded was most probably both stories were partly true.

Berrwynn thanked them for his good advice, and now fully equipped and riding a fast horse and a packhorse in tow he proceeded due south, and after negotiating the steep ridge of Blaen Wenlych eventually arrived at the Great Rock north ford.

He found the battalion encamped beyond the river, and introducing himself to the commander, Berrwynn requested joining the party, the commander and in need an educated person to converse on the long journey gladly welcomed him.

The commander's name was Ebron; a legionnaire from Corinium, and like most present day Roman citizens he was not wholly of Roman blood, and though he professed a Christian, his mother was Hebrew originating from land of Egypt. They became exceptionally good friends, and in their long conversations Ebron revealed he also worshiped his mother's Unnamed God, but was unsure whether it was same God of Christian teachings, but Berrwynn could not enlighten him.

The young military party were in no hurry to reach their destination and totally opposite to their sober mission of going to a war became a festive atmosphere, and their comradeships uplifted Berrwynn's low spirits.

The weather stayed continually warm and they camped each evening by the river, enjoying the fishing and hunting of wild geese for their food, and young recruits whenever possible visited permissive maids or peasant's wives in nearby villages.

Within a few days they had reached Caerwy constructed on an ancient Celtic river crossing, many of city's residents had adopted the Christian religion and it now rivalled Holy Glas Ynys in the Mendip.

The Caerwy hierarchy however were extremely dictatorial and they greedily extracted toll from passing travellers for use of the ford, fortunately Ebron's battalion were on the eastern bank and had no need to cross. Had also sufficient provisions and took of no expensive lodgings and preferring to sleep under the warm summer sky. But on their leaving; Ebron had great difficulty in compelling the local maidens whom had flocked to see the young warriors; as to return to their city, as definitely needed no camp followers'.

Ebron was familiar of this land and leaving Caerwy decided to shorten the route by travelling along a stony ridge way to

Corinium, the now Romano/British capital, after replacing Caerwen which had fallen to the Saxons.

Their journey along the low hills was also enjoyably peaceful and with plenty of wild creatures to hunt and eat, and also had numerous farms and fortunate bread was available. Berrwynn thought how different these people's lives were to the undernourished mountain dwellers where he came from, and descending low hills they came to prosperous Corinium.

Having not before visited Corinum; Berrwynn found it immensely grand, and was crammed with warriors resting after recent battles, spending their time drinking, gambling and whoring.

Alike all Roman cities were mostly Christians and the only tongue heard was latin, and Berrwynn deplored the loss of their ancient Celtic language, its culture and also of their Celtic pagan religious beliefs.

Corinium also contained the cream of well-armed Roman Legionary Guards and hosts of mercenary warriors but despite these safeguards he found the inhabitants were in constant fear of Saxon invaders. A great number of the hierarchical merchants and other's whom afforded, had deserted the city, travelling to the river crossing city of Caerloew, and some even further to Caerleon in Siluria.

Aware of Tarran's strict observance of Roman military ethics Berrwynn was awed to again meet his uncle and whom he had not seen since he had left for his home over five years earlier. And having broken his promise to return with the new intake he now humbly apologised that he had taken him so long to return.

Long military engagements had taught Tarran much of battle strategies and as his name and meaning 'Thunder' was attributed as to his constant tirade of the hierarchies' purely defensive rolls. Despairingly and to no avail, Tarran had constantly emphasised that unless ceased constant defensive roll and instead adopted attacking attitudes defeats would surely continue.

He had assumed his robust tirades had been in vain, but following death of war overlord Tarran was selected to replace, and urged to practice his prospective ideas of aggressive warfare.

Thereafter, and in hard fought campaigns Tarran's now attacking army successfully dislodged the enemy and recaptured fortified chalk hills camps, and with Ebron's fresh contingents drove the Saxons back and to near Caerwen.

The old and trusted warrior Tarran increasingly suffered from effects of his many battle wounds, and though sound of mind he was physically deteriorating and to the dismay of his many faithful followers he suddenly collapsed and died.

Though a professed pagan, such was he admired that his body was ceremonially carried through the hills to lie in the Christian centre of Holy Glas Ynys.

Berrwynn inherited his trusty sword and he was also proud as to wear Tarran's old legionnaire helmet, however replaced its Roman eagle emblem for the fiery dragon motif of Cadwaladr the Great of the Cornovii tribe.

After their commander's tragic departure the hierarchy of the combined Roman and Celtic armies gathered yet again to choose a new overall military leader and plan what Tarran envisaged. Of raising a tremendously larger army and finally drive the Saxons back into the southern sea.

However, with Tarran gone there came disagreements within the combined armies, and firstly whom be commander and also between various factions over the future course of the war. Now the enemy dispersed some envisaged were in permanent retreat and the war ended. But the mostly pagan Cernwy and Cambria warriors strongly opposed those' ideals and believed their gods were crying for a revengeful slaughter.

Berrwynn's military training taught him that only good war strategies brought victories, but this time he sided with aggressive factions, reasoning that enemy's setback was temporary. As Saxons' past triumphs had afforded them of lands and riches and human kind successes' always enhances further appetite for conquests.

Berrwynn feared the Saxons would imitate previous invading Romans military expertise of five hundred years earlier; in gaining access to the western sea at the Severn estuary. Then similarly at the Deva estuary and separating allied western Celtic Cernwy and Cambrian peoples and also Brigantians into weakened independent factions, and defeated separately.

Whilst in Corinium, there continued the inflow of fleeing people, refugees from the central plains bringing worrying news of another mighty enemy called Angles. And whom thet claimed were advancing westwards, killing, raping, and burning farms, settlements and even cities.

Though knew very little of Angles, they were aware of their skill of forging swords of steel, and own iron armaments were of no match to enemy's sharper hardier swords and more resistant to dents.

It was also difficult to prevent enemies advancing across the plains as has very few natural defences, however there were wide rivers but flowed eastwards and defensively of little use, instead advantaged the enemy as their advancing routes. The Angles also benefited in the use of the constructed Roman roads connecting the main cities and simply following found no difficulty in discovering new areas in which to rob of their treasures and destroy.

Berrwynn was now twenty-seven years old and considered a veteran, and with no family ties he was proposed as their overall leader, but before he had decided whether accept the honour, he was delivered a long delayed message.

It came from Rhiannon informing that his stepfather Antwyn had died, and conveyed her deep concern as to their safety from invading Angles, and whom were claimed destroyed settlements as near as fifty miles east from Virconium.

Also repeated that as she was ageing found difficult to single-handedly control the young tribsmen, and dearly wished he would return and installed their leader.

Berrwynn revealed the letter to his comrades and they became extremely alarmed as to vulnerability of their families located on edge of the plains, and foremost in their minds was to immediately return home and safeguard.

The mostly Romano/British Camwy and Virconium warriors urgently conveyed that their first duty was to protect their own families, and pleaded Berrwynn to command an immediate return.

Berrwynn called a conference of all his army personnel; and as he was also in agreement it did not take much persuasion to bow to their wishes, and they all hurriedly prepared for an ever urgent departure.

Within days the northern Cambria and Romano/British contingents were in the process of bidding their fellow warrior's farewell, and at the time little realised it was the last time they would see them.

The returning party decided to travel through the wild western mountain regions, and not only for their safety but also combine their journey negotiating with tribal leaders they encountered requesting their aid in probable future combat.

Calling on their gods for guidance Berrwynn and his fellow warriors embarked on their journey, firstly travelling along the Ermin Sreet to Caerloew; southern-most crossing of the Severn. Where the Romans firstly erected a fort to guard the river crossing of their western road into their city of Caerleon in Siluria

The native peoples feared and loathed the inhabitants of the two estuary cities of Caerloew and Caerdeva as of their previous exploitationand to a degree of slavery enriching their merchants. Therefore within these two despised city's precinct it was wiser to converse only in the latin language, and as to avoid delaying conflicts the warriors inconspicuously slept in low taverns and stables.

Early the following morning the warriors were relieved to leave the confines of

Caerloew, and thereafter crossed the Severn and headed north-west through the vast woody countryside of scattered tribes of Gwent; Romans called the Silures.

Berrwynn was greeted with much ado in many settlements they encountered, the Silures of Hir-wy valley were famous for their skilled long-bowmen, and their leaders promised full support in future conflicts.

North of the Silures lands on Honddu River lay the settlements ruled by Brychan; and meaning Freckled, Ireland born leader and father of the Christian Brothers Berrwynn had associated in Maifod.

Tales tell Brychan initially landed in Dyved and by his Irish charm he gained the daughter of the king, thereafter he usurped and became their king, building his stronghold amidst the Vaan Mountains. Brychan claimed he was commanded by Padriag to convert remaining British pagans, most of his many children became missionaries andwho travelled the lands converting the populace to Christianity.

On meeting, Berrwynn learned that three of his children had but recently suffered martyrdom at the hands of pagan tribesmen, and amongst were his eldest Cynog, and also his much loved daughter Tydfil. The Christian Brothers in Maifod had often spoken of their sister Tydfil's gentle holiness, and Berrwynn was aghast that members of his own pagan people had murdered such gentle persons.

Brychan was known for his generous hospitality, and besides of his great grief he prepared a feast, but Berrwynn and his warriors were in great haste and regrettably they had to tear themselves away from the celebrations.

Leaving Honddu they continued their journey northwards through unknown lands of difficult hilly terrain and warily entered lands of Llyr or Lear of Maesyved. The notorious chief was reputedly distrustful and in disputed with all neighbours, but nevertheless tolerated Berrwynn's warrior contingent and for a few silver coins he provided them with food and shelter for the night. But he gave no definite promises of military support or aid in any future conflicts.

Continuing their journey north they rapidly approached southernmost part of their homeland, and news of their homecoming had already reached their people and they were met by a large number of relieved rejoicing people.

Thereafter were escorted home in triumph along lanes garland with flowers to the Garth of Burgedin and where again welcomed by his mother, and his siblings.

Later, Rhiannon related the difficulties they had in finding Berrwynn to inform that Antwyn had died, they did not know where be found or if even still alive.

Meanwhile twin brothers Geraint and Llewelyn were beginning to acquire an appetite for power and as still under age Rhiannon had somehow keep the peace.

Finally, she had to bow to popular demand; conceding that if Berrwynn failed to be found within a year she would consider setting up a process of selecting a successor, but meanwhile she and alone would remain in command.

On meeting local elders and invited chiefs of neighbouring tribes Berrwynn found that they were all extremely worried by tales of the invading barbaric Angles, as they had been told by 'plain's people' seeking refuge.

CHAPTER IX

<u>BERRWYNN PREPARES FOR WAR</u>

Berrwynn considers defences. Return of Emrys of Tannat. Berrwynn Overlord. Braan joins Berrwynn. Alun Mabon, Gogeran treaty. – West Saxons capture Corinium, Bath, Deorham Caerloew and Silures'. – He spells out his war strategies. Mithras' gloomy predictions. Finally, assistance of Brigantia.

When prospected their defensive possibilities Berrwynn despaired when weighed their possible options and secretly debated. Whether; as when came confrontation was wiser to flee to the safety of the mountains than face inevitable annihilation.

However, gazing across the valley at opposite hills he was reminded of Caradog; and who long ago heroically stood against the overwhelming might of Roman legions; and contemplated what would be his reaction in their present situation.

Pondered whether would stand and fight whilst the same time put his people at terrible risk resisting the now invading Angles, and finally concluded that he most probably would stand and fight.

Berrwynn was cheered when was approached by Ambrosius or Emrys; the retired Roman legionnaire he previously met in Tannat, offering his military experience, and following detailed discussions both agreed on most of their ideals.

In that their only hope of resisting, or even possibly defeating the enemy was by forming a united front of the Roman Legionary Guards and Celtic tribal warriors. However they realised the difficulties of combining these two opposite elements, but it had been successfully achieved against the Saxons in the south.

Berrwynn was fairly optimistic he could persuade his own tribes' people, but whether Emrys could also persuade Romano/British citizens of Virconium and Camwy of the benefits of combining was a problem he could not contemplate.

In event of a war, the inpossibility of defending Virconium was not missed by Emrys and sadly acknowledged that his native born city would probably have to be abandoned to the enemy, and colluded with Berrwynn that it best temporarily hidden. Confirming it was unlikely the Romano/British citizens would agree to such a radical action; and thus possibly prevent the forming of a combined force.

Emrys visited the cities to meet their hierarchical leaders and found the task of persuading them to unite was not so daunting, as had envisaged. As the citizens having heard refuge seeking people's horrific tales were alarmed and grateful of whatever possible salvation.

Having agreed to forming a combined force, their only constraint was choice of overall commander, as their great leader Artuis was now very old, and his only possible successors lacked real war experiences.

Artuis was Romano/Celt of Cornovii descent, and a devote Christian he never indulged in immorality of Virconium, and instead held court in old Camlann fort. Gwenllian, his wife was born in Gogeran and a sister of Gogeran leader Tudor, and in her youth a great beauty attracting many admirers and some say lovers, and now middle aged retained much of her beauty and still also her admirers.

Romans having always been leaders, and their citizens asked Emrys to lead the combined force, but he reasoned that the younger and Caerdeva military trained Berrwynn be their best leader. Emrys' choice; astounded the citizens and they were only persuaded otherwise by him revealing that Berrwynn was also nephew of their much admired warrior Tarran. And that he also would be proud to serve under his command, thereafter Berrwynn was installed overall commander.

When young legionnaire; Emrys had comrades whom later became commanders and hierarchical citizens of varied Roman cities including Brigantia, and therefore he was an ideal envoy to encourage forget prejudices and form a common front.

Meanwhile Berrwynn gathered together experienced warriors and draw plans as how to attract as many field helpers to build sound defences to repel the enemy.

Braan; on learning that Berrwynn had returned from southern wars and longing to see him, travelled to Burgedin to greet him and also discus their Carrog warriors' involvement in incoming war.

When again met they warmly embraced and with uncontrollable tears Berrwynn spoke of his great loss of Tresoara and soon Braan also shed real tears for his sister and sympathy for his friend.

In aftermath of chosen overall commander Berrwynn strategically knew had little chance of winning battles unless were enforced with many more warriors, and was prepared to meet whomever. Friends or past foe; and who could in any way assist in their possible forthcoming struggle. Also unconnected tribes and who were not immediately at risk by endeavouring to persuade that when conquered and lands seized, asserted that their own lands would next fall to enemy hands.

North of Camwy stood a rocky hill, and on its summit a very important fort, and further north on flank of a prodigious terrain overlooking the great plain lay also the great earth built fort of Gogeran.

Possession of these forts was strategically vital in Berrwynn's defensive plan to prevent the enemy encirclment of Camwy and therefore he was anxious to meet Alun, grandson of Burgedin's old enemy Onnwyn of Yale tribe.

Post departure of the Romans; Onnwyn had occupied Middle Deva, Berrwynn's grandfather Cadwallon then warred to recover, and though fighting had long ceased there had been no peace declaration, and constitutionally were still at war.

A conference was arranged with northern tribe leaders at the Gogeran fort to consolidate support of the allied tribesmen, and approaching the great earthen fort Berrwynn viewed their shining 'Owl' emblem, in morning sunshine.

Bards relate that the large oak carved emblem was originally the ancient Dragon of Cadwaladr; the legendry king of Cornovii.

When Christianised, Romans viewed it a pagan idol and set it on fire, and though its great wings had been burnt away it was not entirely destroyed. Its black charred remains resembled perched owl, and mockingly called Black Owl.

As time passed and its origin forgotten was again deemed respectable, but now insect ridden it was annually lime washed, resulting its transformation to their shining 'White Owl'.

When Berrwynn arrived at Gogeran disappointedly found the old fort poorly fortified, however their aged leader Tudor optimistically gave his full support and there followed the discussions with all of the gathered northern leaders.

On meeting Yale's leader Alun ap Onnwyn Berrwynn was impressed in that he had also resolved to fight the Angles; and alone if need be, and they developed an exceptionally good relationship.

When Berrwynn expressed desire of their long delayed peace treaty Alun gladly accepted also a tripartite military pact with their both old Romano enemies. Furthermore agreed to Berrwynn's requests appertaining to the two vital forts of Gogeran and Craig Dhu, and he promised some of his own warriors as to enforce, but momentary the details were as yet to be resolved.

Berrwynn also needed the assistance of northern tribal leaders to protect the outlaying points too far from Camwy to protect, and began discussion with them.

Notably absent was Cenwyn Heer leader of the Halkyn tribe, called Scourge of Caerdeva; as he vented his peoples' suppressive sufferings under the Caerdeva hierarchies in lead mines of their native mountains.

Meanwhile in the south it became what Berrwynn had worst feared, unsurpassed Saxons appetite for victories and continued to Roman Bath and in a great battle killed Berrwynn's successor Coimail. Thereafter in the battle of Deorham they disastrously killed also his successor Condidan, and reaching the Severn estuary captured the poorly defended Caerloew.

Intoxicated by their unbelievable successes crossed the Severn and their sudden advancement surprised and defeated the

Silurians, and gaining the fertile Hirwy lands occupied the Hirwy-ford crossing settlement.

The disastrous outcome robbed Berrwynn of promised Silurian enforcements, but some; and bound by their promise travelled through the mountains to his aid, and enforced on way by outlawed Maesyved tribesmen whom opposed Llyr.

Also to Berrwynn's aid appeared hordes of young volunteers excitedly eager for an affray from little known tribes of the mountain hinterlands, and untrained had no thought of consequences of war. Berrwynn feared that these undisciplined tribesmen who became drunk on druidic drugs for battle, in that they would be more a hindrance to his commanded trained warriors.

Braan as promised returned with a large contingent of Carrog tribe warriors from Pendeva, and though military trained by Antwyn were untried in battle, thereafter Alun Onnwyn also arrived with a number of his promised Yale warriors.

Berrwynn also welcomed a number of retired Roman legionnaire generals and with own private armies offering their assistance, and now his combined force increased to seven thousand warriors.

More accurately comprised of eager combatants lacking battle experiences, also had little or no armour and possessed only few war-horses.

As weapons of war were in such a short supply Berrwynn begged armament merchants of Camlann and Virconium to quickly supply what arms they had, and for iron smiths to hurriedly forge more weapons.

Roman military hierarchy and Celtic warrior leaders gathered in Camlann to plan their defences and forthcoming action when the Angles' expected attacked from across the plains. Their great difficulty lay in anticipating where the enemy chose to attack, and having personally experienced Saxon's battle strategies Berrwynn addressed the gathered generals and sharing of his knowledge.

He relayed that Saxons were fond of following rivers and likely also Angles, and that they instinctively avert fighting in unfamiliar ground such as woods or mountains. Alternatively, chose and often won battles on open plains and where they excelled in hand to hand fighting techniques, and as a race were immensely ingenious at grasping all possible presented opportunities.

As none other had such positive reaction; Berrwynn explained his own strategies, outlining his main plan of strongly fortifying Camlann and west or inner bank of Severn's long curve. And if necessary as far as Caerwy ford, however suspected the Angles dared not venture as far south as they had no wish to confront their also enemies; the Saxons, and now occupying Severn estuary.

Secondly, he proposed a central positioned headquarters at Wenlych and armed with a strong reserve of fast horse warriors and which could be quickly dispensed to re-enforce any weakened embattled sections.

Thirdly, to prevent Camwy position encircled from the north he proposed a strong military presence stretching directly northwards along the Avernwy river from its confluence with Severn. Thereafter continue along the foothills to the Deva river and held by warriors at Craig Dhu and Gogeran forts, further north along Deva river be strongly guarded by Alun Onnwyn.

Beyond Alun and directly towards the estuary was to be guarded by nearer living Cilcain, Halkyn and the other small mountain tribes. Roman Caerdeva already selected to independently defend by own Legionary Guards under Commander Justin Prado.

Ending with sombre note Berrwynn proclaimed the strategy was achievable only if their meagre military numbers and critical lack of arms afforded defending the long defensive barrier lines.

Everyone agreed his battle plans were effectively sound, and the usually critical retired Roman legion generals ceded that in the circumstances was best any one could contrive. As no one else offered such constructive plan it was agreed and steps were taken to prepare its execution, and tribal chiefs lay their trust and life of their warriors in his hands, and earnestly prayed for victory.

For the next few months there was great activity along the Severn as thousands of people including women, children, the old, and even the disabled battled against time building fortifications of stone, earth and wood along its long inner banks.

More and more fleeing inhabitants of the plains arrived and with anguishing tales of murder, rape and wanton burning destruction of cities, villages and of farms.

The effect of the harrowing tales on the population were twofold, some proposed they immediately flee, but the hardier and in learning of their terrible atrocities became more determined to stay and revenge the carnage.

The general attitude was they more feared fighting the barbaric Angles than the Saxons, as the latter were reputed to spare the lives of women and children.

After a long winter of preparing and anxious waiting, and when signs of spring appeared pagan priests informed the gods had predicted that the Angles would soon invade, and in mighty battle Britons will be glorious victors.

Though mainly Christian, Roman cults such as of Mithras were also secretly worshiped, their priests oppositely forecast a defeat and of mass slaughter of not only warriors but also women and children. Furthermore, their cities and settlements would all be destroyed and civilisation the Romans had introduced would be then ended.

Their disastrous prediction caused alarm and commanders became uncertain of some warriors continued support, but strong disciplinarian Emrys dire warned whoever contemplated the prospect of certain defeat.

Recent news revealed Angles were a mere thirty miles or so away and on were on direct course towards Virconium, henceforth their citizens were commanded to immediately evacuate to Camlann fort.

Though had long come to realise their city was indefensible and eventually they had to abandon, but when the inhabitants were ordered to leave argued that as there were no enemy in sight it was not yet necessary. Some concluded the Angles might never attack and sack their city, however they were forced and the non compatibles were assisted to further flee west to the safety of the hills.

Fleeing incompatibles of Caerdeva faced having to beg sanctuary from previously oppressed and revengeful Halkyn tribesmen and Justin asked Berrwynn to use his influence to allow some of his people into safety of tribal hills. Thereafter Emrys and with warrior Celynen was dispatched to try and pacify the hostile tribesmen, asking them to allow women, children, the old and disabled sanctuary, and finally succeeding, but some refuge seekers had already died.

After the agreement Emrys continued his journey to Manceinion requesting their needed enforcements of Brigantia warriors, and taking the threat of Angle invasion seriously and constructed fortifications from second estuary to the long central range of mountains. Placing their best warriors to guard their homeland they eventually agreed to his request, but they offered fewer warriors than was requested. Manceinion Brigantians were known for their dislike of rival Caerdeva, and who referred to them as the greedy slave bearers, and derisory replied. "The overfed citizens of Caerdeva should get off their arses and provide the needed warriors."

Emrys returned to Camlann with promise of assortment of legionaries, but it was less than he expected and in all only totalled seven hundred warriors and possibly many also inexperienced. When informed the generals of low number of warriors and there was much gloom in the camp, but having reached present preparedness they decided they had no option than continue.

Considering the enemy's attacking possibilities Berrwynn greatly feared that the Angles might occupy the undefended plain stretching north from Camwy to the Deva estuary and there possibly capture Caerdeva.

Thereafter if crossed Severn west of Camwy would encircle the Britons in their main bastion at Camlann and furthermore cut Britons' from Burgedin and also their escape access to the hills.

Until he knew the extend of expected Angles attack Berrwyn placed himself at the central position beyond the natural ridge near Wenlych village, and carefully monitored easternmost bow of the river and the most likely place of initial attack. If instead the Angles entered the northern plain, he himself intended to command the vulnerable area beyond Camwy as to vitally prevent their encirclement and also preserve his family in Burgedin homeland.

Planning the layout of the armies defensive positions, Berrwynn and assisted by the commanders selected and as far as was possible that each tribal division fight near their homelands as urgency to protect own people would spur ultimate effort.

Starting at the northernmost reaches, Justin's Legionary Guards independently commanded Caerdeva and the north western estuary regions of the Deva River.

Command of patrolling and safeguarding the long Deva river frontier and the foothills was divided between Cilcain tribe, and Cenwyn Heer of Halkyn, and assisted by friendly warrior contingents from Brigantia.

Immediately to their south Alun Onnwyn strongly defended meandering middle Deva, and combined with a smaller Maengwyn contingent occupied a difficult defended vulnerable gap between Deva River and Gogeran fort.

Refortified Gogeran and containing highly trained Manceinion Roman general and commanding numerous Brigantian Celtic warriors were at plains' forefront.

Craig Dhu hill fort was to be held by Braan's horseback contingent guarding vulnerable lower foothills and western bank of the Tannwy and Avernwy rivers' to its confluence with the Severn.

The legionnaire Emrys commanded Camlann citadel and nearer parts of Severn and brothers Geraint and Llewelyn with own army patrolled the most important point of the river's eastern curve and where firstly expected enemy's arrival.

Gronwy of Talwrn; husband of Aurian was centrally placed at Blaen Wenlych stronghold where has a natural high woody ridge, and a great horseman he led a large well armed fast horse warriors for dispatching as to wherever most neeBerrwynn with the main Celtic and Romano/British army awaited the outcome of the angles attack before deciding which position best engaged.

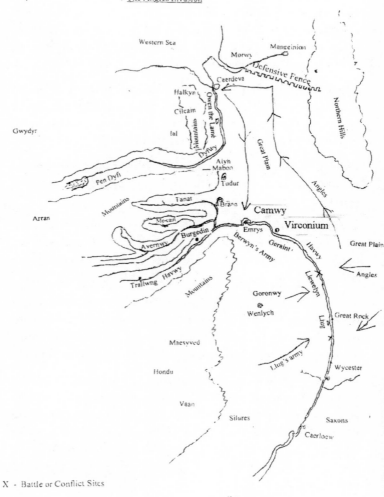

The Angles Invasion

Western Sea

Mangeinion

Morwy

Defensive Fence

Caerdeva

Halkyn

Northern Hills

Cilcain

Owen the Lame

Gwydyr

Ial

Dyffry

Great Plain

Alyn
Mabon

Pen Dyfi

Tudur

Angles

Mountains

Tanat

Brann

Camwy

Arran

Me-cain

Vironium

Burgedin

Emrys

Geraint

Great Plain

Avernwy

Berwyn's Army

Hawy

Angles

Trallwng

Hawy

Mountains

Llewelyn

Goronwy

Great Rock

Wenlych

Llug

Maesyved

Llug's army

Hondu

Wycester

Vaan

Silures

Saxons

Caerloew

X - Battle or Conflict Sites

Estuary

120

CHAPTER X

<u>WAR</u>

The Angles attack. Hard battles fought. Geraint is killed. Angles attack Camlann.

Traitor Llyr. Llywel. Berrwynn addresses generals. Camwy abandoned. Berrwynn leads into battle. Rhiannon Barrier. Berrwynn falls in battle - Oblivion.

Invariably, invaders have the advantage of assembling warriors' at their most advantageous positions and whilst defenders are doubly inhibited of having to thinly disperse their warriors along all possible invading positions.

The Angles' invasion finally began, their numerically superior and well armed skilled force arrived at the Severn at its easternmost curve, and where first tested military the strength of the combined Romano/British defences.

Their first objective however failed, in that were solidly repelled from crossing the river, firstly by Llewelyn's army; and who proudly claimed honour of first victory. In a further attempted crossing the Angles were yet again repelled; and this time by Geraint leading his warriors, and two brother commanders rejoiced that had they were victorious on first encounters.

Their triumph however was due mainly to renowned Silurian and Maesyfed fast delivery archers whom seriously hampered enemy's attempts at fording the fast flowing river. Highly exhilarated the young commanders prepared to rout the enemy, but accompanied Roman veterans feared a trap and advised not pursue. As beyond rivers' open plains they had no certain protection of a barrier, and the young commanders then ceded.

About ten miles further south; and at where the outstretched British defenders were weakest, the Angles gained the west riverbank and some defenders killed and the others were forced to flee for their lives.

It was only through the surprise arrival of Llyr of Maesyfed's army was the situation saved, and for his triumph he was granted commandant of the southerly defences, and thereon he occupied a cliff-top fort overlooking two major river fords.

Having a far superior number of warriors afforded Angles to divide their army, and leaving a substantial force as a consistent threat to the Britons along eastern bank of the Severn the main army proceeded northwards towards great estuaries. Finding Brigantians strongly entrenched behind well fortified barrier the Angles turned their attention to the walled city of Caerdeva., similarly Justin's legionary guards fiercely resisted its walls breached and again withdrew.

Justin's prevention of Angles capturing Caerdeva was highly commendable, but it now became what Berrwynn most feared when spies reported that the enemy had now reverted southerly.

The Angles avoided the heavily forested middle Deva region guarded by Alun Onnwyn and was obvious were now heading for Camwy, and they were later reported to be fast approaching and with only the marshes to slow their progress.

It was absolutely vital to prevent Angles crossing the Severn west of Camwy thus surround and isolate their stronghold and which would lead to the early defeat of their combined armies. This put the British generals in a quandary as whether to withdraw warriors from eastern banks of the Severn as to increase numbers resisting the Angles in the north/west region. But withdrawing warriors not only weakened the eastern defences and inviting further attacks, but also their hasty action would convey their desperation to the enemy.

Therefore it was decided instead to perilously face the Angles without increased number of warriors, and to use their one vital advantage; that of their familiarity of the territory.

The Angles and Britons were lined on opposite banks directly facing each other across the flooded river and each hesitatingly awaited other to venture across, and

Berrwynn was highly concerned whether river's high flood level would continue. He now begged the goddess Powyse to intervene and continue in high water to prevent the stronger enemy crossing and snatching victory, and his prayers deemed answered. The river remained high and though fordable in certain places it was with difficulty, the strong fast current slowed the enemy's progress and becoming easier targets for the British archers.

Geraint; and brimming with confidence after his initial repellence of the enemy; and though he had never met Tarran; venerated, and having heard Berrwynn quoting his warring proclamation. 'To boldly attack, before yourself is attacked'.

He and gainst all Roman taught military discipline; handed his command to his general Syswallt, and led part of his army to vulnerable Camwy section and immediately led a direct assault across the river.

Alas Geraint failed to mount the opposite river bank and tragically many warriors were killed or wounded, and though a foolhardy risk it nevertheless brought the battle into action.

Having rebuffed Geraint the Angles sensed victory and rushed to cross at thought now weakened point, however previous unseen long bowmen now lined the bank and when enemy were in midstream easily massacred.

The Angles retreated thoroughly disarranged and Berrwynn's fast cavalry crossed the river and was followed by their full military force and successfully establishing a bridgehead.

Within hours most of Britons' army was firmly installed on the north side of the river, and triumphant faced the Angles across a marsh. But when Berrwynn saw the enemy far outnumbered his own; and aware of their superior arms and of their highly trained hand fighting skills, he hesitated to immediately attack.

It was credited Berrwynn made the first of a series of errors in delaying to attack, and instead dispatched fast horse messengers to Braan at Craig Dhu commanding him to strongly attack the rear of Angles' army.

It seemed a wise precautionary decision; but proved otherwise, as momentously attacked the disarrayed Angle's was claimed they would have been victorious, as the delay allowed the enemy time to reorganise.

Riding along the riverbank, Berrwynn discovered that his half brother Geraint had been killed in his attempted river crossing, but in war there was no time for grief and he continued along two-mile long line of warriors.

Berwynn assured them they were on verge of victory; and warriors whom were waiting for his signal to attack were impatiently infuriated at his delay and began mutter their dissatisfaction of his over-cautiousness.

Heavy rain had fallen overnight on the western mountains and the overcast skies threatened rain, locally however remained dry and towards midday a very bright watery sunshine broke through the black clouds.

Berrwynn noticed that the sun's blinding glare shone directly into enemy's eyes, and thought it was an exceptional opportunity to launch an attack, challenging his accusers of his over cautiousness he no longer waited for the reinforcements.

He ordered the Britons to surge forward, and for second time he had made a fundamental error. He had not anticipated that the sun's glare and blinding the Angles, also reflected off their highly polished shields and equally affected the attacking Britons.

The commenced battle was fought long and hard, and as was expected there were many casualties on both sides, and though inferior in numbers Britons steadfastly held the Angles. Eventually it was noticed a commotion to rear of the enemy and was correctly assumed that Braan's army had arrived.

One might conclude Braan's inclusion would lead Britons to immediate victory; but battles are not always won wholly by might of men and arms but by also the basic instinct to survive. Discovering surrounded; the Angles like cornered beasts, fought with unequalled vigour and drove Britons back across the Severn, and Braan also to beyond the Avernwy.

The Britons only consolation was in that their Angle enemy halted at the river bank, and probably hesitated as not repeat previous massacre by long bowmen when defenceless midstream.

Back on the south bank of the Severn, Berrwyn gathered his generals together to assess the disaster which befallen them, and was crossly asked – "As why, and when winning the battle, they were now in retreat?"

In their disappointing defeat, the best the much exasperated Berrwynn could do was to contemplate of what would be Tarran's counter-action in such situation.

Angles and Britons were again faced eye to eye on opposite banks keeping their guard, and in dire need to rest there remained an overnight lull in fighting, but when the dawn broke the weather became atrociously adverse. The constantly threatening rain now came down in torrents and further increased already high river level of previous downfalls on the distant mountains.

Berrwynn was most thankful, and floated wreaths of flowers thanking the pagan river's goddess Powyse.

Betrayal

Meanwhile nestling in Craig Vawr guarding the two river crossings Llyr became increasingly incensed with the slow progress of winning the war.

Reflecting if of Berrwynn's victory; Llyr jealously contemplated that without his personal involvement he could not access Angles' gold, and contrived of how he also could achieve a worthwhile share of the riches.

The only other gainful course was a connivance with the enemy, and consulting his blood related three generals he put to them a question. "Could we not possibly gain a greater reward from Angles than await Berrwynn's meagre generosity"?

In finding his generals agreeable he further suggested, "Should we not conspire a pact with Angles and thus gain an advanced deserved reward"?

A general who spoke Angles' tongue ventured across the river bearing a white flag, initially apprehended; but when delivered the traitorous proposition he was dispatched to their hierarchy. Suspicious it was an enemy plot they firstly argued amongst themselves and finally concluded was a worthwhile risk if led to victory over Berrwynn.

The Angles hierarchical leaders informed Llyr that he would be highly rewarded, with stewardship of new province between the Severn and the hills.

Llyr greedily accepted, and anticipating of Berrwynn's defeat gloatingly depicted Burgedin would soon be within his awarded province, but it is doubtful whether the Angles would have kept their promised reward.

Their secret deal was to extract guards from the De'an or South ford and signal fire lit to inform the Angles their passage was clear, and in having long and impatiently waited they were delighted with this bloodless path towards victory.

Berrwynn was unaware of the treachery until a messenger came from their central cavalry position at Wenlych informing of Llyr, and to halt their advance Gronwy had withdrawn to a defensive line along the steep edged Blaen Wenlych.

Llyr's desertion and combined with the much reduced number of warriors due to recent heavy casualties caused Berrwynn to re-plan the overall strategies, and momentary his main army remained rested whilst the river was still in high flood.

Few days' later warrior contingents were seen gathering on Baston Hill south of Camwy, and much to Britons dismay conformed to be Angles, and who by sheer numbers had broken through the defences and had rapidly advanced north.

The Britons had possibly war on two fronts, and feared surrounded and entombed within Camwy, and Berrwynn had now re-enforce Llewelyn's contingent army to withstand their new enemy from the south

Meanwhile; and unknown to the Britons, the main northern Angle army foresaw an opportunity of capturing of Camwy, ingeniously and unseen by cover of trees they secretly rebuilt one of the destroyed Roman bridges.

Completed, would provide them unlimited access into the citadel, and fortunately the near finished bridge was spotted and was immediately seized under darkness. Thereafter combined British warrior contingents under Emrys rapidly advanced across the unfinished bridge and gained the marshy north bank and before most Angles were aware of their foe's discovery.

The course of the war was now again in Briton's favour and gained much ground, but in heavy mud both armies struggled without any one side gaining substantial upper hand. So exhaustive; even paused to re-group and battle became stalemate, and seemed the side with most survivors be victors. When dusk approached and their many dead on the battlefield numerically inferior Britons were noticeably losing ground. Thereafter became an undignified retreat to Camwy , firstly a few carrying the wounded re-crossed to safety of the city, and when defeat became inevitable more and more came and became impassable due to the sheer numbers.

Finally the commanders had to control the narrow passageway and allow only the walking wounded and those whom carried invalids to cross, and causing some to risk drowning wading the river, but preferable to their certain death by Angles' swords.

The final defensive act performed by the survivors within the Camlann bastion was the destruction of the newly renovated bridge, and a decision the Britons did not take lightly as it may have been of a future asset.

After losing another important battle, Berrwynn despondently feared unsuccessful combat would cause warriors to target his overall command, and if they lost their confidence of him the combined factions might break up.

He decided his best course was to be completely honest with the warriors, and in again ask their support to resolve present serious predicament, and gathering his followers together Berrwynn spelled out their options.

He began "At the moment, and to our favour, Llewelyn, Gronwy and also Bryan ap Beibio armies are holding southern Angles at bay, however if the river waters reduces northern Angles will surely attempt to cross and thus surround Camwy.

If successful, Llewelyn and Gronwy's armies will also be separately surrounded, or alternatively if Llewelyn and Gronwy retreat within Camlann it would then allow the two Angles' armies combine and stronger to overcome the defences.

Though you proud warriors; and especially of Camwy may otherwise think, if the city is surrounded will inevitably eventually fall, either by force of arms and men or alternatively by slow weapon of starvation".

Berrwynn's stark declarations caused a stir and alarm amongst the listeners, and again gravely continued. "Whilst Severn is conveniently in flood our escape to the west is but temporary open. Therefore I propose that we withdraw upstream and find a new position to our advantage, and launch another and a final attack".

"Proposing abandoning Camwy I understand is a great wrench to its inhabitants, but our situation is so grave there is no other course of action; unless any one of you can suggest a better strategy we may follow?"

The solemn announcement caused a stunned silence and followed by whispered mutterings amongst the warriors, and Syswallt who succeeded Geraint arose and alone vehemently opposed the plan. Stating he would rather die than abandon city of his birth to the enemy, and to prevent a rebellious division. Emrys personally intervened, announcing that because of their serious situation they had no alternative than accept the desertion of their city.

Thereafter rebellious Syswallt was relieved of command and was heard of no more, and plans to evacuate the city were now carefully prepared.

Many native Britons had never lived in a city, but momentary were pleased with its protection but uncomfortable within its narrow confines and longed be nearer their homes and fight battles within reach of their safe woody hill retreats.

Meanwhile, it came to Llewelyn's notice that the southern Angles were fighting on two fronts and it seemed a mysterious force had joined in the war, and had he not been Christian would have believed that pagan gods had come to their aid.

It was later revealed that Maesyfed warrior contingent on learning of Llyr and his generals' treacherous actions had rebelled and eliminated their leaders, and under their new leader Llywel they decided to return to Maesyfed.

When journeying homewards, they contemplated of their reception when was learnt they had murdered Llyr, and by narrow margin reconsidered previous decision and decided to try and amend their leader's treachery by rejoining Berrwynn's struggle.

Not knowing the present state of the war, they blindly headed north following the Roman road and passing through a narrow valley they saw in the distance the Angles' in combat, and with who they later discovered were Llewelyn's army.

They had now two options, whether to manoeuvre around and join the others in Camwy or alternatively and alone and with fewer and mostly untried warriors to attack rear of Angles army. Considering they were advantaged by nearby hills to escape if failed they decided on the latter and launched an unexpected attack to rear of the army.

Unexpectedly acquiring a new enemy Angles had now to fight on two fronts, and reversing parts of their force against Llywel, conveniently caused a pause in their northern line, and Llewelyn savoured opportunity to withdraw most his warriors. The remaining but a much reduced force were placed under Gronwy of Talwrn who held a much-weakened line and few were expected to survive once southern Angles defeated their new foe's inferior army. Soon; under superior Angles' pressure Llywel was forced to retreat into the hills bordering the plains, and entrenched in familiar type of territory proudly held the Angles at bay.

Camwy was meanwhile painstakingly evacuated and Britons' army now rapidly retreated westwards alongside southern bank of the Severn searching for a secure position where they could make an ultimate stand against the enemy.

In getting nearer Burgedin and without finding a worthwhile defensible position was worrying, and on reaching Avernwy/ Severn' confluence' it became their last resort and chose it as the final battle site.

However, in assessing confluence's potential they found surprisingly and to their benefit, as not only afforded them each individual river's shallower crossing it had also other strategic advantages.

Braan already held the western bank of Avernwy, and Britons' aligned along the southern side of the Severn the Angles in their cramped position between the two joining rivers would afford British archers easier targets.

Satisfied with the chosen battle site Berrwynn prayed to native gods for a victory, and wreaths of flowers were again placed on river waters thanking their mother goddess Powyse for continuing to provide them with high flood water level.

Witnessing Britons' westward retreat; the northern Angles army as were expected followed their realignment along the opposite bank, and reaching Avernwy river confluence, they and too late, realised their disadvantaged position.

To somehow rectify they attempted an immediate surprise attack a little way east of the confluence, but misjudging the Severn's strong current struggled to cross, and again they became easy targets for the British Silurian archers.

The Angles withdrew, but thereafter the Britons were surprised when an Angle contingent then crossed the Avernwy with ease, and fortunately were halted by swiftly reinforcing Braan's army.

In a way this was fortunate, as in seeing Angles easily forded the Avernwy and so could they the other way, and leaving enough force with Llewelyn, Berrwynn; and leading his main army, prepared for the final battle.

Whilst archers on southern bank of the Severn showered arrows at the Angles and Braan likewise on west bank of Avernwy Berrwynn's army were protected as successfully forded the river. By sheer determination they managed to drive their opponents before them until came to a flooded marsh, and beyond Angles stood on a bluff realigning their army.

A lull followed whilst Berrwynn assessed of how to approach their encampment across the unsure ground and hindering a cavalry charge, alternatively be a facial hand to hand sword and spear battle and of which Angles famously excelled.

When news of defeats reached Rhiannon she put aside grieving loss of her son Geraint and contemplated what assistance she could provide Berrwynn. Anticipating that he mostly needed re-enforcements she sent urgent messages to outlaying tribes pleading support to launch a reserve defensive force.

Their response was far better than she had expected, however only the very few had any military training and those who had, had no previous battle experiences.

She also sent a message to rival tribe of Maesyfed, and receiving no immediate reply, Rhiannon presumed were uninterested.

Berrwynn with his main army beyond the Avernwy knew nothing of the several hundred strong but poorly armed elderly men, young boys and amazingly widows revengeful of Angle slain warriors whom had gathered upstream of the Severn.

Some who heeded the call thought Rhiannon was too old, but having heart of a lioness she led the march downstream, and sight of such numbers firstly alarmed the Britons and were indeed relieved to discover were own people.

A few days later and much to everyone's surprise another civilian army arrived, and the newcomers were discovered to be from Maesyfed; and who also heeded the call to arms.

Leading the new arrived contingent was Marchell the young widow of their late leader Llyr, and not knowing of Llywel's re-entry in the war had wished to amend their dishonour she recruited a civil force to aid Berrwynn.

Marchell pleaded for her tribe's forgiveness, and Llewelyn forgave, but Aurian and who presumably lost her husband Gronwy through Llyr's treachery, vowed that she would kill any surviving members of Llyr's family.

Llewelyn was saddened by Aurian's stance, and to evade recriminations when fighting a war he rescued Marchell and she stayed under his protection at his camp on south side of the river Severn.

It was Rhiannon suggestion that they erect a strong defensive barrier completely across the valley, and all available personnel were employed to hastily construct, and when complete it stretched across the valley from Avernwy to Breiddin Hills.

Whilst in Breiddin they encountered Bryan ap Beibio with a small guerrilla army, and whom after defeat of Gronwy had carried on fighting in the hills, activating so many enemy warriors it gratefully eased pressure on Briton's southern flank.

Meanwhile Berrwynn leading his whole main army continued to charge the enemy without positive signs of progress, and finally before the light faded they comprised all their available warriors to make a great final effort.

Under heavy horses and thousands of struggling feet the fighting continued and it turned the already marshy ground and into a blood ridden quagmire.

Amongst the frantic melee, Berrwynn's trusty grey stallion was disastrously felled beneath him, and he had now no choice than carry on fighting on foot.

He no longer could see to command the battle and knew not of its progress, he and with sword and shield he fought overwhelming opposition, and soon came to realise it was very unlikely he would survive the bloody battle.

The last recalled was feeling a tremendous blow to side of his head, followed by searing pain in right shoulder, his legs began to fail and he helplessly collapsed into the muddy and blood soaked earth.

Berrwynn tried to regain his feet, but was impossible as a tremendous weight pressed down on him and seriously restricted his breathing, and moments later visualised Tresoara holding out her arms as to embrace him.

Then total blackness.

There ends the story of Berrwynn's mortal life

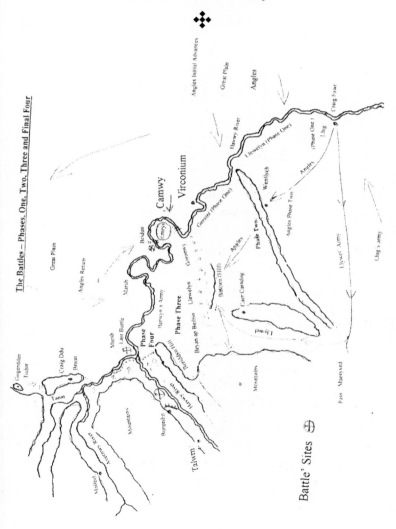

CHAPTER XI

RETURN TO CYNWEDYN - ANDROSSAN'S TESTIMONY

Tells of post Berrwynn's departure. Battle is lost. Rebellion. Emrys overlord. Aurian Warriors triumphs. Angles retreat. The war is ended. Commemorations. Emrys controls borders. Llewelyn marries Marchell. Powysland Reinstated

Having told his life story Berrwynn was extremely anxious to learn the fate of his remaining family members and tribes' people post his departure, however if was detrimental he debated whether best remain ignorant.

Berrwynn became unable to bear the uncertainty of their plight and eventually pleaded Androssan reveal and whatever was the outcome, and anticipating he would eventually enquire Androssan was prepared to testify their circumstances.

On the designated morning Androssan was sitting as usual on the boulder below the great waterfall quietly meditating, and sensing Berrwynn's arrival he slowly opened his eyes, smiled and greeted the troubled warrior.

Generously partaking of the tongue loosening wine Androssan wiped the spilled dregs off his beard, his face now sombre and looking deep into Berrwynn's eyes warned "What I am about to reveal is not to your best expectations, however it outcome secured independent existence, and more than enjoyed under Romans."

The Aftermath - Contemplating all was lost' the bedraggled survivors of Berrwynn's army were intend on seeking refuge in the western hill valleys and when achieved Avernwy's west bank discovered a well manned fortified barrier.

Its presence confirmed that not all British resistance had collapsed and greatly lifted their spirits, and they were soon welcomed by Llewelyn; and who informed that he had now inherited their leadership.

Though ceded he was possibly a good peacetime leader, but when also informed he was now also the overall military commander they were unsure of his ability. As in their fierce war of survival they feared his passive nature was incompatible to their blood spilling struggle and dissatisfaction mounted and spread, and nearly all vociferously asserted their disapproval of his command.

In attempting to regain their trust Llewelyn pledged the engagement of extra warriors; but when they discovered his promised intake was untrained civilian volunteers' they again rebelled. As to the shouting and abusive calls Llewelyn's oration was largely unheard and their leaders furthermore treasonably declared they would no longer obey or fight under his command.

The situation became so serious Emrys was called to dispel, however was self solved, Llewelyn's leg wound he had acquired in battle again troubled him and unable to mount a horse was deemed incapable of leading an army. The rebellious warriors however sceptically believed he was only face saving.

Thereafter overall war commander fell to warriors' popular choice of Emrys of Tannat, and though ageing he was highly reputed, as he had proved in defence of Camwy.

His appointment cheered dissatisfied warriors and harmony was restored, and a true legionnaire Emrys honoured its traditions and discipline, and when acquired overall command he arrested the ringleaders of the dissenting warriors. Substantiating his position he subsequently hanged warriors' leaders as example to others under his command and who might again protest and at his command

Having now lost many warriors, and also very short of arms they could no more renew as were mostly produced in Roman cities Emrys called a meeting of military commanders to review the future course of the war.

Their overall conclusion was that they were never likely to recover the plains but with the advantage of woody hilly terrain they could possibly withhold the enemy from further expansion.

As Burgedin was now also vulnerable to an Angles attack it was decided that its residents be temporarily evacuate to comparatively safety of the further westward settlement of Talwrn.

Berrwynn's sister Aurian was distraught at probable death of her missing husband Gronwy and vehemently vowed to avenge, and discarding all Christian beliefs she reverted to the blood letting paganism of her ancestors.

The young firebrand was not alone as her strong personality had attracted her many followers and included were similar widows as was herself.

In Celtic warring tradition women were of equal status and Aurian formed a fighting force kown as Widdow Warriors, and were fearlessly earnest in their task. They swore to revengefully fight regardless of dire consequences and if suffered a glorious death it earned the ultimate; Nevol; of their Celtic beliefs.

However women held no part in Emrys' military campaigns, and considered if they foolhardily bore arms it would result in their wholesale massacre, and he as overall commander strictly forbids their involvement.

His inherited Roman demeanour of women's military capabilities wildly outraged Aurian, and she promptly reminded him of the Celtic warrior queen Buddig's triumphs over earlier Roman army rule.

Emrys wildly underestimated the women's sheer determination of inclusion in the affray, and tired of their continued persistence; he and to pacify, allowed them to guard the now vacated Burgedin Garth.

Aurian was unheeded by his patronising gesture as she had further inspirational plans and seriously accepting the task, and firstly she ordered the erection of another barrier at the approach to Burgedin. When completed was topped with sharpened forward facing stakes, and encouraged helpers to gather as much as was humanly possible of highly combustible gorse, deadwood and dead bracken.

When an enormous pile it was lined a short distance behind and parallel to their barrier and hemming defenders in between thus preventing any retreat, conveying to the enemy of their earnestness to fight to ultimate victory or to their deaths.

Victory or Extinction

In the long dragged out war both British and also Angles warriors were extremely tired and to a point of exhaustion, and Emrys expected the enemy commanders delay further attacks until their warriors were rested.

Aware of emergence of British's reinforcements and instead the Angles staged a presumptive charge before effectively mobilised, fortunately the Britons were able to hold until fully enforced by their civilian volunteer forces.

The Angles were now also in need of reinforcements and commanded their southern army contingents to abandon fighting Llywel and also Beibio's army in the hills and join their main army along the Severn Havwy.

Their again massively newly combined Angles army attacked and drove Britons back and beyond their impregnably thought Rhiannon barrier, and even to verge of Aurian's barrier guarding Burgedin.

Now near end of British resistance, but women warriors concealed behind their barrier with their bodies starkly painted in blue woad and white river clay and hair of red ochre and animal blood awaited a signal to attack.

Night approaching and helpers were ordered to light the highly combustible barrier behind the barrier, and when raging flames lit the darkening sky Aurian called her warriors to mount the barrier. Standing against red sunset and immense roaring fire behind them, the women and naked to their waist they displayed their infernally painted bodies and wild flowing red bloodied hair.

Their sudden horrifying satanic appearances and inhuman screaming traumatised the tired half-crazed Angle warriors and fearing were confronting avenging Celtic deities hesitated.

The momentary uncertainty was the women's opportunity, and regardless of survival and with unmitigated ferocity mercilessly hacked, cut and thrust the half mesmerised enemy.

The women's frenzied attack also shocked Emrys, but the surge was what he needed and enforced by newly arrived Bryan ap Beibio's and Llywel's armies, and civilian volunteers; they now and for the first time outnumbered the enemy.

Emrys now also also forced a massive onslaught with entirety of their combined British forces successfully forced Angles to retreat and well beyond the Rhiannon barrier and towards Camwy.

Though the river confluence meant to be their last stand, Burgedin battle proved otherwise and won by the courage and sacrifice of the brave Aurian's Warriors. But as their initiative dwarfed the male warriors; the women's place in history was discreetly suppressed and unrecorded.

Though Aurian's Warriors achieved maximal vengeance, but sadly; and as Emrys predicted, most of their numbers were horribly massacred, and among the dead lay their leader, the ever courageous Aurian Wyllt

Virconium was wantonly destroyed and abandoned, and Camlann became the Angles military stronghold and in which to guard the bordering lands.

Though rejoicing Britons claimed a great victory it however was mostly hollow as the plains and Camlann citadel were lost, and raising an equivalent British force to dislodge was impossible; or at least in near future.

History tells the Angles' had no ambition of combating native Britons amongst their familiar woody hill valleys, and ironically Rhiannon's barrier across the valley exactly fitted as their manageable western border.

The war over, survivors; but minus many brave warriors and also some of their leaders, now began to return to their tribes, and former Romano/Celtic peoples and who could not now return to their cities had to integrate with tribes' people.

To mark end of the war Golwelan came to bless the fallen and four giant crosses were erection on the battlefield in remembrance of four prominent dead leaders, Berrwynn, Geraint, Aurian Wyllt and her husband Gronwy.

Neither Berrwynn or Gronwy bodies were ever found, but Geraint was reburied in Maifod, and Aurian's still war painted body was buried with fellow warriors on the banks of the Severn; as be near the Mother Goddess Powyse.

Is doubtful Aurian would have approved of Marchella erecting a Christian church over her burial place, when later sanctified it became a place of pilgrimage.

Braan of Carrog whom successfully held the line along the Avernwy was last to leave the battle ground, and with his warriors remained to bury the dead, and eventually they also returned home to Pendeva.

The Burgedin tribe's decided to permanently remain in Talwrn and with Emrys of Tannat, thereon guarded their defences, and apart of minor infiltrations it remained almost peaceful.

Llewelyn; the only male survivor of Rhiannon's children married Marchell the tribe-less young widow of Llyr, and as to regain their self-confidence reverted the tribe's name to their Celtic pre-Roman name of Powysland.

Llewelyn and Marchell brave attempt of tribal re-affiliation proved otherwise, as instead of their marriage cementing relationships with Maesyfed, the legacy of Llyr's betrayal long remained.

The union of Llewelyn and Marchell brought forth a son and whom they named Brochwel and he after his father's death became a good and powerful leader and his rule brought peace and fortunes to a renewed Powysland.

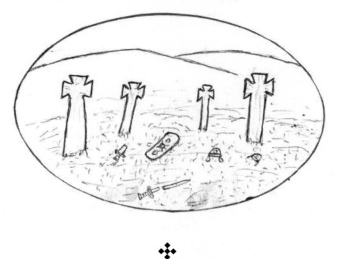

Chapter XII

Chronicle of Oenone
or Nonn the Blessed

*Berrwynn grieved for his family and comrades and was relieved
not all perished, and though the war unsatisfactory ended realised
could have been much worse.*

Berrwynn was enthralled with Androssan's revelations of
post his departure, and also anxious of learning of his mother
Rhiannon and adorable sister Oenone, and again Androssan
agreed tell their thereafter life story.

Androssan however had very little to declare of Rhiannon;
only that she lived into a good old age, and in her advanced
years became a devout Christian and enjoyed a deservedly
restful life with her son Llewelyn in Talwrn.

When eventually died she was ceremoniously buried in Holy
Maifod besides her husband Antwyn, and very near her later
reburied warrior son Geraint.

Thereafter Androssan declared was now going to narrate the
life of Oenone; and who became known as Nonn the Blessed,

and of her determination to establish a Christian mission in Pendeva, and most of all of her mysteriously conceived son.

Oenone, meets 'Roen. The Great Synod. Golwelan secures the holy relics, but dies and are lost. Nonn builds her church. Dervel and Deiniol. Braan returns. Nonn pregnant, baby is born. Flight to the estuary, Roen is presumed killed.

Nonn meets Braid, and she blesses her baby, Dewi.

When completed his usual meditation, Androssan whilst prepared to relate their story extracted container of wine, and pouring into two goblets he handed one to Berrrwynn; and gulped the other whole.

Oenone had also become a devout follower of the Christian teachings and subsequently was enrolled in the church in Maifod, and later installed a Sister in the Faith.

Oenone; and now natively called Nonn, and whilst in Maifod she encountered a young bard who earned his living visiting tribal settlements to entertain the populace. When discovered his name was Roen she recalled Berrwynn speak of this remarkable young bard from Pendeva, the two became friends and conversed a great deal. In questioned Roen revealed that he had alwys wished to be a bard, and a proficient player of his father's harp since young and becoming acclaimed, entertained whosoever paid for his services.

The Angles having conquered the plains, and the near presence of their reputedly savage neighbours perturbed the poorly defended Britons, and continually feared that they would eventually attempt to invade their hill valleys.

Christian Brothers were also concerned for the preservation of their churches, and especially their near border Mother

Church in Maifod, and as how best safeguard it was decided to call a synod of church leaders.

Firstly, they had to establish members of synod, decided on original Brothers and Sisters missionaries, and followed by most merited converts who established new mission churches. However Cynog, Illiog and Garmon the Younger were too far away to be contacted in the limited time, and were unfortunately excluded.

Imitating the number of the Lord's disciples, twelve leading members of the diocese were chosen, and the aged and wise Golwelan was selected as non voting senior adjudicator of the Great Synod.

As expected their main topic; the future of near border Mother Church in Maifod led to heated discussions over a proposed suggestion of re-siting Mother Church well away from the present border.

Most devoted members were horrified professing it was unnecessary as their Lord would surely protect, however after much debating were eventually outvoted in that it had to be moved to a safer location.

However it was a difficult decision as to which of the new mission churches it be relocated and which led to more heated discussions, thankfully by the following day the number of outstanding locations was reduced to two.

Myllin's church in the Cain Valley, or the Burgedin/Powyse new tribal settlement church at Talwrn. Obviously Myllin, also Garmon and Dogfan reasoned that Cain Valley was centrally located and not easily accessible to the heathen Angles.

Cadfan strongly opposed, stating had to be Talwrn, as the location was protected by the now located Powyse warriors, and after seemingly endless debate the majority decision was to re-locate to Talwrn.

Golwelan, and whom had said very little throughout the proceedings, and when the decision to move Mother Church to Talwrn was about to be agreed he slowly arose from his chair, and laying aside his bridle roll he extolled own judgement.

Proclaimed that he; as honoured keeper of the holy relics, and alone responsible to the Lord for their safe keeping, and thereon, that though protected Talwrn was was also vulnerable. - Even more so, when the Angles learned of their treasures.

The synod was extended to discuss Golwelan's objection, and Myllin was now convinced he was about to grant her church the holy relics. But to her surprise; dismay and then anger, he also rejected reasoning it was no further from Angles' border than was Talwrn.

Though Nonn was no synod member she approached the Brothers and suggested that Roen; and in having greatest knowledge of hidden valleys, he would surely know of a safe place to keep the holy relics.

Synod members were now tired and grateful of any solution that would allow them return to their families; but were doubtful Nonn's suggestion that of an untouched location would break the deadlock. As was their duty they requested Roen's assistance; and not mentioning the treasured relics enquired of him. "Where; and beyond reach of Angles', could they build a shrine to their God"?

Roen as his father was a thoughtful person and needed considerable time to asses' problems however the following day unexpectedly returned declaring he knew of such a place. An almost hidden and difficult to penetrate valley and surrounded by mountains of treacherous peat bogs, accessed only by acknowledged guides.

Golwelan was intrigued with Roen's description of the valley, and commented it   was possibly the Lord's chosen place, and at his great age of four score years he and against all advice planned to accompany. However was resolute to personally oversee the installation of the cherished chalice and other relics in a safe haven before he died.

Following Golwelan's ultimate decision they now discussed as whether to also move the Mother Church to this valley, but because of its remoteness; not one delegate was persuaded, and instead opted for their former choice of Talwrn.

The Brothers; and who also greatly venerated the holy relics, grieved at their loss and especially their monetary worth in attracting pilgrims, but as they were Golwelan's sole responsibility, had no say as where he decided install.

Thereafter they planned the Mother Church's move to greater safety of Talwrn, and where built a larger church also called Mair, and Tysilio, a local born convert, chose to stay in Maifod, and he became the redundant church's patron.

Myllin was piqued that Golwelan had not chosen her Cain church to install the relics and subsequently refused to accompany her father on possibly his last mission. And Braid, his younger daughter, and who was already tasked caring for the old priest gladly accepted, and her friend Nonn also decided to accompany.

On the holy day commemorating the risen Lord, they bid farewell to their friends, and guided by Roen and with three well armed trusted warriors to guard the treasures, they departed on their long and difficult journey.

Roen avoided the acknowledged way and he led the party along Heilyn Way; an ancient track used for transporting lead, and which twisted and turned through unknown hills and vales. As they had to consistently assist Golwelan to negotiate steep gradients their progress was very slow, and when finally

148

crossed a barren mountain pass they beheld a deep valley, and was the threshold of holy Pentanat.

To reach they had to somehow convey Golwelan across a marsh and on finally reaching marsh's end they tiredly sheltered under a craggy cliff in a most delightful dell.

Golwelan was satisfied the valley was a secure venue to install the holy relics, but exhausted and feeling unwell he instructed others to continue to a distant church, and that he would shortly follow after he had rested. Unaware of his critical condition they left him to rest alone at the dell and continued on their way towards; and what they learnt was Garmon the Younger's own mission church.

Golwelan later staggered into the church gasping for breath clutching his chest, and hardly audible he spoke of the treasured relics.

It was assumed he said to have wrapped the holy relics in straw and placed them in a cleft in the cliff where sheltered, but before he was able to reveal the exact location Golwelan collapsed and died.

The pious senior Christian Brother was solemnly laid to rest within the encircled confines of the site of Garmon's crude stone and reed roofed church and duly proclaimed a Christian Celtic Saint.

Despite desperate searches of the numerous crags the precious holy relics have remained undiscovered, and became known as Craig y Caregl or Chalice Rock. Centuries later Melangell chose to also dwell in this very dell prior to the building of her priory, and legends say that she recovered the relics and installed them within the priory, and leaving a hidden clue.

A 'symbolic hare' portrayed on the church's rood screen, in the Welsh language a hare is 'ceinach'; and which also means precious objects, and when Melangell was confronted by Brochwell was said hid 'ceinach' in under her flowing gown.

Golwelan's grieving daughter Braid returned with the warrior escorts to Maifod, but Nonn had no reason to return and continued her stay, and in the company of Roen she assisted Garmon in his pastoral work and care of the sick.

In the evenings Roen entertained them with songs accompanied on his harp, and when informed he was soon going to visit his father in Pendeva; Nonn enquired whether could accompany him and enabling her visit her cousin Braan in Penllyn.

Roen and rapidly falling in love with Nonn was delighted that she trusted him to accompany across the lonely mountain passes, and he immediately granted her request.

A week later the two climbed the steep track to the mountain summit and passing the dreaded bog called Pennau all was quiet and nothing was seen of the legendary mysterious flying object said within. Continuing along the track they passed through summit gap of Enflamed Pass, and legendary carved by the flying fish's collision and thereafter gouging a great scar and causing the bog. Descending the other side of the mountain they passed a deserted citadel where Nonn's forefathers' Carrog people survived Roman rule, and thereafter they endlessly followed the long straight valley and at last arrived in Pendeva.

On reaching Penllyn settlement they discovered that Braan had not yet returned from the war, and in his absence Enfys his wife ruled, and as her name; and meaning 'Rainbow'; was also of many colours - or moods.

Highly neurotic; Enfys feared that young warriors planned to depose of her, however was unsubstantiated as most tribe's people respected Braan and tolerated their sad situation until he returned. Enfys also feared strangers and Nonn's arrival was of no exception, but Roen reassured her that the Christian maid was no threat, and that Braan was now also Christian.

Knowing Roen of old Enfys trust trusted him, and she granted Nonn permission to build a Christian mission church in Penllyn, and with high hopes it was named Llan-fawr or Great Church.

The Carrog tribes people came to admire and revere Nonn and as to her gentle beauty believed Nonn was embodiment of Mai; their goddess of fertility.

In this vast pagan wilderness missionary work was huge, and Nonn was soon in dire need of pastoral assistance, and when told of a sea coast cell of Breton missionaries she had thoughts of pleading their assistance.

However Roen informed it was near three days' journey, and very dangerous as since Roman road guard forts had been abandoned was frequented by notorious road thieves.

Nonn; and though afraid, adamantly assumed the good Lord would protect her, and when Roen realised she was now determined to travel to the Western Sea he dutifully offered to escort her, and she gratefully accepted.

They began their long journey, bypassing the first estuary and by end of the day arrived at the second estuary and stayed the night at a Cernwy priest mission, and the following day arrived at a third estuary and without once viewing the sea.

There was no problem finding the Breton Padarn's large Mother Church and in meeting the priest Nonn explained that she needed experienced helpers in her work in Pendeva.

Her timely arrival was a miracle Padarn prayed for, as the Bretons had made very little headway as clumsily had impressed Christian moral rules on the unwilling tribes' people. The pagan tribesmen much enjoyed their physical pleasures, and in Christians forbidding their long held practises they became hostile, and now the missionaries were now afraid to venture far inland for fear of their lives.

Nonn; and native born, also relative of a leader could hopefully offer them access to the interior tribes, and Padarn gratifyingly granted her request by offering two of his most trusted missionary priests.

Dervel Gadarn, was a Celtish prince who had fought at Camlann and sickened of the killing gave up his sword for a wooden cross and became a Christian missionary. The other priest was a Breton called Denoual or Deiniol in Britain, he was a highly educated scriber and worked at writing Holy Scriptures in Iwerddon until came desirous of returning home to Brittany.

However, Deiniol's ship was shipwrecked on the Cambrian coast; and in miraculously surviving he assumed the Lord had sent him to Cambria for a reason and stayed there a missionary.

Within days Nonn, Roen and the two priests were ready and full of renewed hope they began the very long return journey to Pendeva, and when finally arrived the priests were suspiciously welcomed by the Carrog people.

In following months they all tried very hard to deliver their Christian message, but it was not what they had hoped, as tribesmen feared that converting would lead to severe vengeance from native gods.

The two priests became despondent and considered returning to the coast, but having become good friends of Nonn and fearing for her safety they felt obligatory to stay for a while longer.

Their decision proved wise, Braan, finally returned from the war, and offered his assistance, and deludingly placated the peoples' fear of deities' vengeances by personally guaranteeing their safety.

Subsequently Dervel and Deiniol established churches nearby and later Deiniol travelled to hostile Gwydyr northern coast to establish more Christian missions. Dervel travelled south to his native Siluria, and established more churches and eventually became Bishop of Menerva.

Within a few score years missionaries travelled throughout the Celtic lands and completed converting its peoples to their faith.

However the same missionaries were too fearful of travelling east to convert the reputedly savage Anglo/Saxons and the unenviable task fell to Augustine, and sent from Rome.

Miracle of Pendeva -Arrival of Dewi

The return of Braan to a childless marriage to neurotic Enfys was little comfort to either and in his various activities involving the Christian mission unavoidably he fell in love with Nonn.

It was not only Roen and now Braan fell in love with the winsome priestess, she and unintentionally acquired a host of admirers, and even the much older Dervel would have also been happy to make her his wife .

Naively, Nonn was surprised when discovered that she was pregnant with child, and realising the implications became extremely distressed and she withdrew from her pastoral work and sought solitude in the woods.

The tribe's people were astounded to learn Nonn was expecting a child and many who adored and revered her saintliness could not accept had mortally sinned, and quoting their Christian teachings. Professed it was surely a miracle, a parallel manifestation of birth of the Lord, and Pendeva's own 'immaculate conception'.

The priests' however were sceptic of a Divine involvement, and confusing the newly converted people, and despite the priests' negativity they remained convinced, and even before was born he was name 'Dewi', meaning 'Of God'.

Inevitably, Nonn's condition created malicious gossip and of adverse discussion amongst unconverted and less devout, and massively assumed the baby's father was Braan, others Roen, and wickedly even Dervel was mentioned.

When Enfys heard rumours of her husband's liaisons; and furthermore that Nonn was expecting a child and when she herself could not conceive, and intensively jealous swore to harm her assumed rival, and her threats were not to be ignored.

Nonn requested Braan's now widowed mother Colwen for refuge at her home in Caer Gai, and though dread Enfys' reaction if discovered, but convinced it was Braan's child; and her own grandchild, she secretly allowed to stay until born.

Behest her host's constant enquiry Nonn still stubbornly refused to reveal of the child's father and of which added to the mystery, and a serving maid declared Nonn was so naively innocent, she did not know herself as who was the father.

Roen wished to marry Nonn, but he and only a poor bard was wary of asking a saintly daughter of tribal leader for her hand, and concluded if he now offered she might assume was only proposing for the baby or pity sake.

But traumatised Nonn had no thoughts of marriage, and though appreciated Roen she was unaware loved her and wished to marry, and ironically if he had had the courage to ask, it is very likely she would have accepted his proposal of marriage.

Eventually a boy child was born, and called him Geraint after her brother, and when the birth became known the devoted amongst their tribe's people however insisted on calling him Dewi, as to their thoughts of his miraculous conception.

Fearing Enfys' threats to take her life and possibly also the baby's, Nonn had now to leave Caer Gai, and Dervel who had given much thought to Nonn's predicament suggested she travel to Padarn's Church near the coast, and seek his guidance.

Nonn was very sad to leave her own founded mission church of Pendeva and also the tribe's people, and again Roen dutifully offered to escort and trusting his strong protective presence she instantly accepted his kind offer.

A few days later with Roen leading a pony and Nonn riding with her baby Dewi strapped to her back they began the long journey to the coast, but barely travelled four hours when confronted by road thieves in narrow gully.

Roen bravely faced them alone, and urged Nonn to hurry ahead fast as was possible, and on reaching a woodcutter's hut she begged assistance, but the old man feared confronting the murderous thieves. Instead he advised her to hurriedly continue to the sea coast, and much distressed and exceedingly tired Nonn arrived at first estuary mission church and tearfully related to the priest her tragic story.

The priest Elltyd organised a party of local tribesmen to search for Roen, but to no avail, and for days after the ordeal there was still no news or of him or the thieves. Elltyd eventually advised her to continue her journey to Padarn's church, and when Roen is found he would be advised to follow her, but knowing the reputation of road thieves; he in his heart doubted was still alive.

A priest called Ilar whom was returning to his near coast church accompanied her on her resumed journey to Padarn at the estuary, and in again meeting the high priest she explained her predicament.

When the elderly Padarn enquired the parentage of the baby Nonn steadfastly kept her secret, and though sympathetic he explained it was not permissible for a woman to live within his church's compound, and certainly not an infant.

Alternatively, he suggested she could live amongst the tribes' people in nearby settlement, but as had no income he inferred it would be better if she found a more conducive home.

The priest Ilar; and who had a church ten miles further south informed that along the sea coast there was recently established mission founded by an Ireland born priestess Llian Braid. Having previously met the gentle motherly Braid; Ilar was convinced she would welcome Nonn and especially the new born baby.

In having heard no more of Roen's fate, Nonn desperately prayed to her Christian God to grant the brave pagan his safety, and vowed that on reaching Llian Braid's mission church she would dedicate an altar to Roen.

The next day they embarked on the journey to the settlement and took them the whole day and they again arrived extremely tired and hungry.

Llian Braid whom never had a child of her own warmly welcomed Nonn and the baby, and taking the precious bundle in her arms she uncovered his head and observed his glowing face and bright blue eyes.

Braid at this moment sensed something exceptionally holy connected with the not long born child, and turning to Nonn she prophesised: -

"This, your blessed baby, I sense his name will shine on earth, as also in heaven".

Oenone, or Nonn the Blessed's Journeys

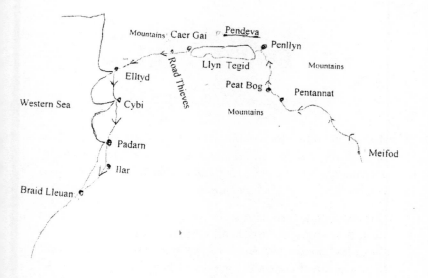

Chapter XIII

Revelations of Androssan

Androssan begins his revelations. Vvisit the silver chariot and tells of Cerys his lost love, and comrade Bruiser Bell. He confesses of Professor Quillan disasters. They visit Androssan's home. Berrwynn is unwell and fears his loss of sanity.

Androssan intended withholding revelations of celestial secrets until Berrwynn was sufficiently recovered from his depressive ill-health however Supreme Gods judged it was more detriment to his health if continued perplexed and decreed he now be revealed.

When the great day broke Berrwynn apprehensively journeyed to usual venue below the great waterfall, arriving he found Androssan in usual transcendence, and greeted he opened his eyes and gratuitously returned the compliments.

As usual Androssan reached for the wine container and poured out two generous goblets of the potent liquid and handed one to Berrwynn. And whilst slowly savoured silently contrived of how to reveal the fundamental secrets to mortal and without its sheer starkness cause alarm.

After a while; and stroking his beard he soberly declared that he was now ready to start, but firstly declared that Berrwynn had to swear a divine oath of secrecy; and formality completed he began by warning. "What I have to reveal is so laboriously baffling, mortals are likely to doubt or even to completely disbelieve. And as not shock your already perilous nervous system I will divulge only a little every day."

With his clear blue eyes penetrating Berrwynn's inner being Androssan firstly conferred a hint of his own phenomenal transition by proclaiming "Similarly, was through a tragic occurrence I also arrived, but was immensely far into the future, and later I will reveal the whole story and cause of my arrival".

Turning to proposed text he continued "Firstly, I have to reveal that your taught Celtic beliefs of reincarnation of man is unfulfilled. As it does not wholly lay in reincarnation but in also pre-carnation, and which is extremely difficult for mere mortals to understand".

Androssan paused to pour more wine, and again continued. "The privilege of entering; and where I conveniently call Cynwedyn, is appointed by the gods, most mortals arrive in spirit, but a few; as you Berrwynn, are bodily escorted from the field of battle."

He again paused to give Berrwynn time to reflect, and then continued, "Mankind has searched the heavens for your' called Celtic Nevol, and I have now to declare that it lies beneath his very feet.

The infinite good Earth that you call Talam; and who feeds and cares for all that dwell on her ample green bosoms is the Supreme Mother Goddess.

Grian the Sun God and Supreme of all deities sheds his invigorating warmth and consummates the Mother Goddess and thereon she brings forth all life, and in simplified mortals' terms Grian is father, and Talam is mother of all mankind."

Berrwynn listened in awe to the revelations and his head began to reel; but was not from continuances of incredible revelations but from his unfamiliarity of the potency of the fortified wine. It now absolutely confused his senses, and seeing his intoxicated condition Androssan ceased his narrating and sent Berrwynn home to recuperate.

The following day; and sorely suffering uncomfortable after-effects of excessive alcohol Berrwynn was relieved when was not again offered the wine, Androssan however poured himself a goblet; savoured and then continued his revelations. "In my celestial messenger duties my mortal presence has emerged in many centuries and many nations.

I served Nebuchadnezzer in Babylon, in Egypt when was built the great tombs and Persian deserts I endlessly travelled with Alexander. I have also beheld Greek philosophisers and great prophets. Moses, Buddha, Confucius and others, and I found that within their own spheres their wisdoms similar".

Androssan's stare became so intent it seemed to Berrwynn as if peering into his very soul but when paused to pour more wine it somewhat relieved the tension, but he then again continued. "I witnessed crucifixion of a said divine and of a saintly maid burnt at the stake, and icily perished in a despot's siege of a nation called Russia. These I quote, are only a few of the many lives I have enjoyed or more often excruciatingly endured, witnessing of mankind's progression.

However, and instead of the horrendous experiences abatating his aggressive tendencies constantly repeats, and culminated in two most horrific wars and involving more nations and people than ever thought was possible.

Furthermore my dear Berrwynn, mankind's ingeniousness is far beyond your uninformed mind, processing unimaginable wonders, firstly steam driven horse-less chariots and of iron ships. Later; and the most difficult for any novice to apprehend he invented winged chariots and which alike birds fly in the heavens".

Berrwynn unquestionably accepted grandiose magnifications of the gods which are beyond mere mortal's comprehension, however claiming that man's ingenuity equalled the gods' magnifications; he found most difficult to believe.

His common sense dictated iron descends through water, and concept of flying chariots was absolutely preposterous. However he hid his doubts or truefully his complete disbelief, as he feared challenging what the Supreme Gods purported.

Androssan continued "In the horrific conflicts chariots of land, sea and of sky were transformed for destruction, brandishing fires of Belial called explosives, and destroying whole cities and tragically causing insurmountable carnage".

The horrendous details of man's bestiality continually increased and it totally sickened Berrwynn and was eventually absolutely confused by the revelations, and in his present illhealth he could not bear anymore. He harbouring thoughts that he was possibly hallucinating or even worse becoming insane, and following day he failed to meet his tutor. And again the day after, and many days elapsed before he was prepared to think about what he had heard, and much loner to again face the ordeal of listening to the revelations.

However, after resting for a few weeks his conscience began to trouble him and he felt obliged to again visit Androssan and apologise for his absent, but secretly he also needed confirmation that his sanity was unimpaired.

When again met; Androssan immediately recognised what troubled Berrwynn, and assured him that he was perfectly sane and referred to what he had previously declared. "I repeat, the revelations are difficult to grasp, but the Supreme Gods insist that it is necessary that you learn relevant knowledge of progression of mankind, and I therefore continue".

As on previous occasions they sat on opposite boulders at foot of the waterfall, and this time Berrwynn was offered; and accepted a goblet of the yellow wine. Androssan rapidly proceeded with his revelations of the horrific tales of mankind's bloody progression, of greed, envy, slavery and butchery of captured prisoners. Berrwynn definitely did not want to hear any more and wished he could shut his ears to further revelations, but there was no way of stopping Androssan's relentless narration.

"Firstly in war, alchemy unlimitedly advanced and many physical diseases were overcome. But man's unforgivable misuse of Talam's ample resources was causing her to deteriorate resulting in the ever ever-bountiful goddess to gradually cancel her contract with mankind.

But man's ambitions had now even out-limited Talam's domain, and from her bountiful greenery he travelled into the cold outer darkness. Firstly to the barren Gelach and later the equally uninhabitable heavenly bodies Romans called Mars, Jupiter, and Saturn".

Accepting no interruptions he continued "Man then further travelled, and far beyond the great Grian to the most distant universes of the gods fervently searching the unknown".

Berrwynn could stand it no more; and interrupted Androssan by asking him to cease narrating for the day, and seeing his anxious condition he apologised and told Berrwynn to leave and rest and not return until felt completely able to accept the revelations.

Androssan tells of his own arrival.

Berrwynn took a long rest, and when eventually returned Androssan's only comment was a greeting, and pouring out a goblet of fortified wine and gulping its contents he leaned back against the mossy cliff closed his eyes and meditated.

His absence seemed endless, and Berrwynn was unsure whether instead had fallen asleep, and a delicate situation he courteously decided to wait until returned to normality.

Whilst patiently waited he scrutinised Androssan's appearance and noticed that his hair was astonishingly indistinguishable from the maidenhair ferns growing from crags behind him. Peering closer Berrwynn observed his face was also of a greenish tinge, and he became perturbed whether was a prodigious revelation, and so transfixed he was slow to notice that Androssan had reopened his eyes.

Observing Berrwynn's shocked face Androssan wistfully smiled and asked had he seen a ghost, but he received no reply.

Wiping his beard, Androssan again resorted to his narration. "I personally travelled on many missions searching for new worlds, and then mortal name was Andreas Sorrenson, and natively unpronounceable was simply called Androssan.

As said, I was born extremely far into the future in a large country across the western ocean; a land unknown for hundreds of years, though I believe a Celtic priest sailed to its edge, but experiencing inhospitable weather failed to settle.

In this great land my father served as a military general, and my mother; born in another vast eastern country was a scientist, a profession known to you as alchemist, and she had come to my father's land to further her career.

I personally embraced not one, but both my parents' professions, by becoming a military alchemist or astronomic physicist studying the mysteries of the universe, and later I commanded a wingless flying chariot searching for other habitable worlds.

In what became my final mission; the sky chariot and called rocket collided with a large flying rock and it developed faults in its navigational controls. Ungoverned faulted its intended course and possibly for years we travelled further and further into a far black oblivion.

Subsequently we became unable to breathe, and one by one my companions died and when I also was on verge of death I saw in far distance a wonderful vision of a most beautiful colourful world. Later I could see its blue oceans, and nearing its rivers and eventually greenery of its trees, a most glorious place and where man could surely live in plenitude and peace.

However, I was concerned that after fortunately discovering this new wonderful world my life would end by being immersed in its oceans, and maybe by chance or merciful act of a god. We headed for a wonderfully green small island and landed softly in a mountainous marsh".

Berrwynn had now regained interest and he became absolutely fascinated and begged Androssan to reveal more of this new and wonderful world, but he had ceased narrating for the day and Berrwynn was told to leave. On departing; and as in afterthought Androssan called back to him "Tomorrow we will visit the ruined chariot and you will see its magnificence, and its very presence will assure you of the truth".

On his way home and also throughout an excitable sleepless night Berrwynn pondered over Androssan's story and of his contradictory account stating that the chariot was near. Whilst previously declared landed in a far off blue/green world.

Berrwynn was so eager to visit the chariot and soon as sun arose in the sky he hurried through the woods to meet Androssan, and discovered he was already there and humbly washing his clothes in the river.

Greeting him, Berrwynn asked whether the journey was long to where lay the fractured chariot and Androssan replied was only a few hours' away, and very soon they started on their journey to its hidden location.

As they travelled along in the morning sunshine Berrwynn's mind continually embarked on the controversies occupying his thoughts throughout most the night, but when he asked Androssan received no reply. Seemingly was abstracted and as if not of this world.

A shimmering lake filled the valley bottom and halted to enjoy the wonderful panorama, and Androssan also stopped and apologised of his absence of mind, explaining he was in deep consultation with the gods.

Pointing to distant hills he informed it was where the ruined chariot lay entombed in a peat marsh, but warned of the strenuous continuation of their journey.

Climbing out of the valley through a steep gully they reached a summit plateau and then clambering through difficult terrain of sodden peat moss and heather clumps were suddenly confronted by what Androssan described as a 'rocket'.

Berrwynn had imagined it be similar to a Roman chariot and was astonished when saw it resembled more an enormous silvery fish and with similar fins. Also noticed it was obviously slowly sinking into the great peat bog, its rear end was already half submerged, and soon it would all disappear forever

Such was it position its entrance faced the sky, and entry was achieved by climbing its slippery side and took a considerable effort to open the door, and when clambered inside Androssan escorted much bewildered Berrwynn all over the vast structure.

Patiently, he explained the purpose of each object and also spoke of his commanding duties, and Berrwynn was absolutely enthralled. And not only with its enormity but also its contents comprising of many indescribable gadgets and obviously mostly damaged. A chamber consisted of metal containers and Androssan professed preserved their foods and regrettably confessed that little now remained, and in another chamber Roman glassware containing liquids, and of which jocularly referred to as his medicines.

As was now getting dark they settled down to sleep the night inside its great body, but Berrwynn was too exited to sleep and continued questioning, but Androssan was now tired and promised to answer all his queries in the morning.

The next morning Berrwynn awoke very early and wandered around the interior of the chariot inspecting every aspect and wondering their purposes, and on reaching a door to the front or cone section he regrettably found inoperable.

Retreating to so-called cockpit he noticed wonderful images of the crew and families and marvelled at their attire, and background scenes of dwellings. Also a number of previously unseen horse-less chariots and which also fascinated him.

Looking at the images he noticed one was of Androssan in strangest of clothes, and on his left side a small slim figure with feminine face and easily mistaken for a maid. On his right side an enormously tall well built smiling figure displaying shiny white teeth, and looking closer Berrwynn observed his skin was black, and unfamiliar he was puzzled, and concluded it must be a god.

Androssan presently appeared bearing cold cooked meat and delicious beer, and whilst they eat he sat in his old commander seat surveying faded images of his comrades, and Berrwynn noticed tears in his eyes. Discreetly wiping them away, he pointed to one of the images and commentated. "Though masculine dressed the one on my left is my dear Cerys, a truly wonderful person and we were to marry when accomplished our mission, and I greatly miss her and her merry laughter. The other, is my long time buddy Bruiser Bell, 'greatest fighter in the Air Force', and we trained together as aviators in Westport before qualifying as astronauts, regretfully was at my request he joined me on this our last mission".

Berrwynn did not know what Westport or Air Force meant but he discreetly asked no more questions as was obvious Androssan still grieved the loss of Cerys and friend Bruiser Bell.

Instead he let him continue uninterrupted recalling his arrival. "I do not know of how long I lay unconscious and on recovering my senses I stayed within the rocket for days regaining the strength in my legs.

Looking out one day I saw two young maids encircling the rocket as if were searching for the entrance, and so pleased to see them I rushed to get out as to speak to them. But when saw me in my astronaut clothes they drew away in fright, howver when I removed my astronaut outer garments and saw I was human they allowed me to approach.

I recall the women were dressed in long woollen gowns and with embroidered ribbons tied around their waist, and I distinctly also remember noticing tips of their toes showing from under their gowns. But apart of their clothes they seemed normal as the girls I dated back home in Burns Wyoming, however when spoke, I knew not their language and neither they mine, and which at the time I thought was very strange.

As in my mortal age all people spoke either of the two international languages, the official American/English or otherwise Mandarin, however through the use of crude signs we eventually established communication.

They became to trust me, informing were sisters called Tannya and Rhewa, and after few days conversant enough as to indicate that they would take me to meet their father --". Androssan suddenly halted; and when resumed he strangely discontinued telling his original story.

"Though conversation was limited the sisters understood my grief and assisted me burying the bodies still remaining in the rocket", and pointing to partly erased mounds Androssan went quiet, and he then walked away.

Surveying the graves Berrwynn found an overturned stone marker, and though he recognised engraved latin letters he however could not read the strange language.

When later questioned of the unknown language; Androssan declared it was English, language of the Angles and Saxons, but differed from original as enormously enriched by conquering races' tongues. Berrwynn then questioned of what became of the Celtic language and he replied became mostly extinct except in the mountainous fringes, but still defined in names of rivers, mountains and of previous established settlements'.

Berrwynn was eager to question the anomaly, and asked "Why; and when flown to a new world the rocket lies here in Talam? Androssan admitted was bizarre and stressed it would take time to palatably explain to a previous age mortal.

The next day they started back to the settlement and throughout the journey Berrwyn reflected over what he had seen and also of what Androssan had spoken, but resisted from asking questions until he was in an obvious mood to answer.

A few days later sitting in the shade of the cliff sipping the yellow liquid previously cooled in the cold rushing water, Berrwynn; and unable to constrain his curiosity came directly to the point asking. "Will you now explain why, that when first stated the rocket had flown to a new world and now it lies in Talam"?

Re-asked same fundamental question, Androssan sighed and taking a deep gulp of wine he once again leaned against the cliff and closed his eyes, when reopened seemed mesmerised and his now facial transfiguration greatly startled Berrwynn.

He knew not whether Androssan noticed his unease, however he seemed unperturbed, and addressing him, began "Berrwynn my dear friend and pupil, I will now try to answer your enquiry of why the rocket; and which travelled far away, still lies here in Talam?

The answer to the riddle is not of common mortal knowledge but of the highest degree of alchemy, and a satisfactory explanation is very complex for those whom are unspecialised. Therefore I ask you to accept a simple equation of the existence of circuitous universe". And stroking his beard whilst searched for appropriate phrases, he then continued, "Far off our intended course, we entered into a then unknown reversible time syndrome; similar to ancient Celtic inter-circular stone carvings, and which may have also predicted similar aspects".

Noticing his bewilderment; Androssan declared "I see my explanations are beyond your immediate understanding, nevertheless as is my duty I will continue.

The wayward chariot travelled into what we alchemists' refer as parallel universe, and unknowingly we had re-entered Talam's circuit, but not at its present time but far back in its previous age".

Looking at Berrwynn's dazed expression; Androssan paused, and continuing he added, "I can see you that even when explained in simplest terms you are totally perplexed, and as not increase your confusion, I will abandon the explanation until another time. However, do not despair, as thereby will come the time when you will be glorified with absolute knowledge of Supreme Gods' secrets, as it is your utmost destiny".

For the first time Berrwynn was now privileged a visit to Androssan's hidden dwelling in the woods, and entering was truly amazed and recognised it was somewhat alike the rocket's interior. Consisted of strange items and of whose purpose continued a mystery to him, and invited to sit down Androssan then pressed a small protrusion and interior was immediately bathed in light.

Out of a metal alcove he produced an effervescent drink, and though the weather was warm its contents was icy cold, and reaching for his potent yellow drink poured a little into the goblet. Declaring it would much improve its quality, and indeed he was correct as Berrwynn immensely enjoyed.

Kicking off his badly worn sandals Androssan sighed then commented, "These are my old astronaut boots, and are the my only items of wear still remaining", and further declared "Having long outlived my clothes I wear what tribes' people provide, and amusingly am often mistaken for a druid".

Rear of the shack backed onto a cavern bordering a rushing brook, and hearing a whirring noise Berrwynn asked its purpose, Androssan declared was a generator, and where made the magic light which lit rooms, and also kept the food cold. Nearby was round contraption and with tubes excluding, and from an outlet there dripped the intoxicating liquid which he poured into their drink. And proudly Androssan declared it was a whiskey distillery he had built, and copied from some backwoodsmen back home whom made illicit alcoholic drinks.

For hours they sat and talked and Androssan related his childhood memories of a place he called 'Good Ole' USA', and about many wonders man had such as speaking; and even passing of moving images to very many miles away.

It seemed to Berrwynn mankind now possessed skills equalling that of Supreme Gods, and he wondered how they reacted to mortals' obvious challenge.

Professor Quillan' Experiments

Resuming austere face, Androssan declared, "As not alarm; I previously omitted certain adverse aspects pertaining to the rocket, and as you are now stronger I will now reveal some unfortunate incidents resulting from the expedition.

You may recall that you were unable to enter front compartment of the disabled rocket as communicating door machinery was inoperable, within the cone section was laboratory containing innumerable objects.

To combat diseases, alchemists had been working on what we call genetics, or simply are variably means of transferring the genes which determine growth of life of humans, animals and plants.

The eminent Professor Seymore Quillan who led the experiments was previously highly acclaimed for successfully eliminating many diseases and becoming exceedingly rich; and with his enormous wealth he financed the expedition.

I however believe he accidentally infected himself and had become insane, and illicitly in his private laboratory unrestrictedly introduced human genes into dumb creatures. Mainly apes; but as you have never encountered are primitive creatures whom walk on hind legs somewhat resembling humans, but fundamental lack human brain.

Professor Quillan is professed was creating an ape/man capable of performing menial duties, intended to populate a world of super humans and with servile apes and other creatures as to await on of all their needs".

Androssan added, "When the rocket collided I was unable to enter the laboratory and contact the professor and his two female colleagues, and is very likely were killed before or in the collision.

It was only later I came to realised there was a great gash in the rocket's casing, and apes and other unknown experimental creatures may have possibly escaped"

Berrwynn was speechless, and unbelievingly stared at Androssan's face throughout his forever increasing phenomenal declarations, and furthermore startlingly continued "There are tales of sightings of half-human creatures having adapted to our environment, large scale-ridden amphibians, and of beautiful maidens in lonely lakes. However these stories are best disregarded as are the usual; bard's created mythical tales".

After Berrwynn's traumatic war experiences and followed by his extraordinary transition to this place he knew not where, thereafter constantly revealed the incredible testimonies; he could definitely take no more.

He felt as on edge of a precipitous cliff, and if he toppled he would descend into oblivion of deepest darkness and with no possible return to sanity.

When explained of his increased anxiety, Androssan sympathetically agreed that he desperately needed much more time for his health to improve before accepting any more revelations and of such fundamental and abnormal occurrences.

Androssan told Berrwynn to leave and complety relax, and only come back when he felt absolutely sure he was ready to face further and the ultimate of revelations.

CHAPTER XIV

SURREAL ?

Berrwynn, dispenses druidic medicine. Enters fantastical revitalisating cure. Absurdities of Peredin. Berrwynn enters a pact with fire goddess Taanwibber.

Cadval destroyed. Taanwibber reappears. Mochan's final but unfulfilled revenge.

For many weeks Berrwynn rested trying to eliminate from his mind his nightmarish visions of horrifying past occurrences also the phenomena's which befell him since he arrived in this mysterious underworld called Cynwedyn.

He had now developed a steep downward spiralling feeling as if was being sucked deeper and deeper into a swallowing bog and without anything to hold to prevent his descent. And despite Androssan's assurance that his mental health was unimpaired, it was so bizarre doubted as whether he had correctly assed.

However, if Androssan's diagnosis was correct he pondered as whether from the start it was a colossal dream or a nightmare and when awoke he still lay badly wounded on the battlefield. There was also a strange third possibility, in that he was already dead; but as yet minus ultimate reward of being amongst his honourable Celtic ancestors.

Utterly despaired he decided to again approach Androssan and plead he dispense stronger medicine, and was even more when found the physician absent and probably gone on a celestial journey, and possibly centuries before he returned.

Absolutely frustrated Berrwynn and on verge of voluntary meeting his ancestors when suddenly remembered that Androssan's surplus initial medicinal compound was stored in his laboratory. And as memorised medicines' other constituents he contemplated as whether he also could dispense, and absolutely desperate he decided he would try.

Though confidently started he soon realised that he knew not the measures of ingredients and deliberated whether wise to proceed and guess amounts according to their potency, and having nothing further to lose, he proceeded to dispense.

He correctly introduced the synthetic compound however absolutely bungled the measures of various plants, herbs and additives especially druids' hallucinating sacred fungi, otherwise it seemed to him he had successfully dispensed the cure.

When took the medicine his anxieties quickly disappeared, slept extremely well and recurring nightmares had completely ceased, and when awoke he felt physically refreshed. Berrwynn was now indeed proud of what he had achieved alone and without the aid of Androssan.

However he developed extraordinary urges, such as to dance sing and peculiarly to dispel his clothes and to run naked through the woods, and the strangest; and a somewhat to his delight phenomenally increased his libido.

Felt as when he was a young man in pursuit of Burgedin maidens, and recalling Androssan professing that he needed company, and he had jocularly added. "The love of a good woman is the most wonderful medicine known to man".

At that time Berrrwynn's only need of women was for nurses, and in now taking his medicine he regularly craved for female company, and hastily abandoning the rood shelter he secured a dwelling in the Maengwyn settlement.

Bronwen secretly yearned for Berrwynn, and when she learnt that he was now amongst them could not withhold her eagerness to visit him, and morning of May Queen festival she appeared at his door in spectacular finery of her festive gown.

Greeting her in the bright morning sunshine Berrwynn shamelessly savoured her voluptuous body shadowed through the diaphanous gown, and following the sensuous display he became overwhelmed with licentious desire of physical love.

Similarly Bronwen's long unfulfilled desires also came to the fore and very soon the inevitable occurred and became lovers, and constantly fulfilled their desires with utter lasciviousness. And neither cared whether Bronwen's aged husband Peredin became aware of their liaison.

However in his highly sustained amour Berrwynn completely forgot to continue his self medication, and suddenly his new found desires retracted and his depressions returned and began to question their relationship.

He could not now discern whether his love of Bronwen was genuine or merely physical attraction after his long and suppressed desires due to his illness.

Berrwynn was much relieved when Androssan eventually returned, and in mentioning his dilemma whether correct to abandon Tresoara for another, the physician smiled and replied. "Believe me, it is destined; your love of Bronwen is no rejection of Tresoara, but compliments, and when finally revealed you will see is true".

Afraid his illness would return; he re-continued his most exhilarating medicine, and could no longer live without its invigorating warm glow enveloping his wounded body, but he dared not reveal of its dispensary to Androssan.

ABSURDITIES OF PEREDIN

It was unconceivable to Peredin that the reason he had no heirs was his own deficiency, and now aged; three times married his latest young wife Bronwen was also childless.

When learnt of his wife's torrid affair with Berrwynn; and though raged but such was the young warrior's popularity he was powerless to act, and instead strove to appear ignorant until he contrived a sure way of ending their relationship.

Eventually devised a plan to get rid of his rival, and firstly he requested Berrwynn visit him, and when met they both falsely greeted each other as loyal friends and whilst remaining deviously careful not offer any hint of the liaison.

Peredin conferred he wanted a warrior to destroy an enormous winged lizard and from whose presence they had long suffered, and Berrwynn accustomed to such myths as purported by bard's depreciatively dismissed. But as not upset their delicate but false relationship he and at appropriate intervals courteously nodded his head as in approval.

Peredin and not detecting his contemptuous disbelief claimed that many attempts had been made to kill the lizard but all failed as its scaly hide is impenetrable, and its confronters were dragged under its mountain tarn. Thereafter their indigestible armour was then spat out onto the banks, and each attempt only increased the lizard's appetite for even more human flesh.

Berrwynn's opinion of Peredin rapidly regressed from that of his gullibility of not being unable to distinguish myths from reality, and multiplied to sheer contempt when declared that whom seen the lizard say it also talks as a human.

Furthermore declared, that the lizard was originally a warrior called Cadval whom fell in love with the seductive river goddess Meinir, but to marry a goddess had also to acquire divinity. To aquire the necessary celestial knowledge the goddess enticed him to drink from their forbidden spring, and which angered the gods and resulted in him suffering their retribution, becoming a great lizard.

Peredin relayed that they fed the creature with sheep, goats and sometimes even cattle and which made the people very poor, and during spring festival it had lurched out of the tarn demanding human flesh. However it was successfully cheated by given an already dead human body, but they feared that next time there might not be a dead body available.

Berrwynn contrived that bards would handsomely pay for the acquisition of such fantastic tales, and though he falsely appeared intrigued he constantly struggled to suppress his mirth. But it also angered him that Peredin so belittled his intelligence; in expecting him believe such nonsense.

Berrwynn was obliged by his Celtic upbringing in the beliefs of the presence of pagan gods, goddesses and to a degree the Unnamed God and which Tresoara had been converted. But he considered existence of a talking lizard was way beyond his or anyone else's common sense acceptance.

But when he compared these outrageous myths against his own phenomenal experiences and that of Androssan bizarre revelations; he had now to concede that Peredin's fanciful tales of a talking lizard was no less believable.

Then another thought entered his mind, and wondered whether Peredin's alleged mythical creatures could possibly be what Androssan relayed of the strange half human creatures which escaped from the collided rocket? Then also recalled when concussed on the misty mountain, he knew not or whether imagined the encounter with the strange dwarfed creatures who spoke as were humans, and compassionately had tended his wounds.

Berrwynn again descended into dark despair and holding his head in his hands he wearly pondered as whether and unknowingly he had deeply offended the gods, and they were now punishing him by setting insurmountable hurdles in his path.

Furthermore Peredin also appeared distraught; declaring that he was beset with worry at extend of lizard's increased later demand; that of ultimate prize of Bronwen, his beautiful young wife.

Berrwynn however was unsure as whether Peredin was merely enticing his participation when also surprisingly declared; that he and rather than she cruelly sacrificed would offer her to whomever was brave enough to face the creature.

Far from being convinced of Peredin's tales of the lizard were true Berrwynn became alarmed that he might somehow loose his love to another and he hurriedly volunteered to personally confront the terrible creature.

In the unlikely instance Cadval did exist Berrwynn's shattered shoulder prevented a physical encounter, and contemplated it was only by guile he could destroy, but however much he thought he could not think of a sure way of slaying.

Seeking advice he was informed that only the fire witch goddess Taanwibber was clever enough to hatch such devious plot enough to deceive the allegedly greatest of lizards.

However he was warned to be careful as Taanwibber she was also extremely evil and she was banished from Maengwyn for bewitched own husband Mochan into a boar for his unfaithfulness with the ever seductive river goddess Meinir.

Apart of Averna's dream visitation, Berrwynn had never met a god or goddess; and he was apprehensive of meeting the fire witch goddess Taanwiber now residing in a sunless dank upper valley.

Berrwynn however bravely stated he was prepared to even visit worst of possible Celtic inferno to rescue his Bronwen, and having metaphorically declared; and when saw the valley he found more than equalled. Desolate silent wilderness and where no birds sang or any living creature could be seen or heard.

Locating the tarn, the presence of a meat eating creature was evident by the stench of rotting flesh hovering over its dark waters, and beyond the tarn he noticed a dark cave entrance.

He had correctly assumed it was where Taanwibber lived, and when neared; he saw her sitting outside stirring a pot, and reflected by the flames her long fiery red hair he firstly admired. But when she turned towards him; his admiration of her was much regressed when now also observed her hideously ugly face.

Seing the handsome warrior approaching Taanwibber quickly transformed herself and into a beautiful and exquisitely back combed fiery haired maiden.

Introducing himself, Berrwynn was invited to sit down beside the fire and partake of a putrefied stew cooking on the fire, declining the food he sat down on a log warming his hands by the fire.

People of Berrwynn's superior status rarely entered the infernal valley, and Taanwibber contemplated it must be of importance, and when explained the reason of his visit, she then led him to a slime covered cove.

Though travelled the long journey Berrwynn still doubted the lizard's existence, and he now and for the first time lay eyes on the great creature laying asleep in the mud, unbelievably confirming what Peredin professed was no myth.

Following what he had seen he had now to emphasis to Taanwibber the rewards would gain if devised a plan which led to the destruction of the lizard, also granted her wish of re-joining the tribe's people further down the valley.

A few days later Taanwibber came to the settlement with a carefully formulated plan of ridding the lizard by its own greed, Berrwynn was intrigued she possessed such wisdom devising such clever plan, and readily agreed to its execution.

The fire goddess having no children, explained she wanted no worldly riches and her reward would be the first born of the tribe after the event.

So eager was Berrwynn and tribe's people to destroy the lizard they all too readily agreed and no one dreamt the consequences of their binding agreement, and they lived to regret their hasty decision.

Taanwibber's carefully thought plan was to erect a large standing stone in a field and encircle with sharply barbed iron rings, thereafter the edifice was dressed in a white bodice and made to look like a maiden prepared to be sacrificed.

When the trap was laid, Cadval was informed that his uttermost feast was awaiting him, and despite Meinir's dire warnings greedily flew down the valley searching for what he was promised. When dawn broke revealed a figure dressed in white standing alone in a field, and ravenous the great lizard licked its dribbling lips and opening enormous jaws, bit. But when attempted to swallow it

resulted in what Taanwibber had so cleverly predicted, the disguised barbs successfully punctured its throat and consequently the life blood drained away staining the stone bright red.

After the successful deed there was much rejoicing, and the lizard's body was dragged through the streets by teams of horses and finally was taken to a high ridge above the settlement and covered with a large mound of earth.

Thereafter the blood stained maen became revered and symbol of Maengwyn people's deliverance, and ceremonies were performed around the now shrine on its anniversaries. Firstly the stone was re-coated red with blood of a sacrificed animal, and flower garland procession carrying a maiden dressed in white led to the grave of the lizard, and on now called Red Lizard Ridge.

Berrwynn was overwhelmed with praise for his genius in saving Bronwen and of tribe's deliverance from the horrendous creature, but Berrwynn's now increased popularity only caused Peredin to be more jealous.

Enraged Peredin was unsure whether had been more desirable be rid of Cadval or Berrwynn. He now planned to have him also killed and contacted Meinir urging revenge the death of her past lover Cadval, and shortly after, the usual shallow river greatly flooded and swamped the settlement drowning some of the residents.

Fortunately, Berrwynn had recently vacated his home for a more palatial dwelling on a hill in preparation for his wedding to Bronwen and miraculously escaped the flooding.

Ironically or was possibly a Devine intervention; Peredin on his return journey was also overwhelmed by the onrushing waters and he himself was also drowned.

There was very little sympathy for the devious old leader; and Berrwynn their saviour and also marrying Bronwen became contestant for leadership and the tribe people were pleased to elect him leader.

Berrwynn and Bronwen were duly married and in a ceremony officiated by Androssan who sprinkled holy water whilst he rendered blessings of the gods, and as tradition they gave him a bonding wreath of oak and holly branches entwined in ivy.

The great feast which followed not only celebrated marriage of their beautiful Bronwen to honourable warrior Berrwynn and also afforded official celebration of their tribe's release from long suffering, and all were invited to enjoy.

In their excitement they forgot to invite Taanwibber, and when merrymaking the now enraged fire goddess burst in amongst them and glaringly stood before the family and guests sitting at the head table. Guests seated below mistook her for a clown and applauded expecting to be entertained, but when realised it was the awesome witch the applause died and a deathly silence prevailed.

They all now sat qiuetly anxiously awaiting Taanwibber's fiery retribution, and the goddess; with hair wildly disarrayed and face glowing red outstretched her arms wide as like a fire encircling the audience, and began her address.

"I Taanwibber; and who you have obviously forgotten in not invited to the feast, and of which would not have occurred but for my wisdom; as the bride Bronwen would now have been devoured".

Utter silence reigned over the chamber's occupants, and sweeping her fierce eyes over their stunned faces Taanwibber menacingly declaring, "The river goddess Meinir is no longer my rival, and now united we are determined that the bond is now honoured".

Pausing briefly, the fire goddess then gravely quoted contents of the bond, "As agreed by your now leader, the firstborn of the tribe be delivered forthwith its born, otherwise forfeiture is pestilence. A pestilence and so forceful it will destroy all the people of your land if the leader as so much sets a foot within tribal land".

Within a cloud of black smoke Taanwibber promptly disappeared out of the celebration chamber, her departure was followed by thoughtful silence as they all contemplated the stark meaning of her threat. In order to forget the gloomy predictions large amount of very strong alcohol was freely distributed amongst the guests and the drunken merrymaking continued throughout the night.

Berrwynn and Bronwen thereafter settled down to an ordinary married life, acquiring land, grew crops and bred domestic animals, and as time past Taanwibber's awesome threats furthered from their minds, and again forgotten.

The tribe's people prospered and within months Berrwynn was now to be a father and was the firstborn of the tribe since their deliverance, and a boy child was born and they called him Maelor.

Suddenly Taanwibber reappeared dragging her be-witched husband Mochan behind her on a piece of rope, wrathfully demanding her promised child or otherwise pay the forfeiture. Her reappearance caused much fear, and tribe's people asked

Berrwynn what he intended doing to rid them of the wrath of the fire witch goddess, and also pacify her evil accomplice, Meinir the river goddess.

For days Berrwynn contemplated a solution but could find none and approaching the gods also brought no enlightenment, and perplexed he tried contacting Androssan to seek his guidance, but to no avail as had again gone through the watery veil.

Berrwynn again journeyed to the odious upper valley and plead Taanwibber to instead accept an increased reward.

When arrived he noticed that since Cadval's departure the valley was now peaceful, and it seemed a picture of contentment. Taanwibber was sitting at the lakeside with her bare feet dangling in the water and affectionately stroking the rough hide of her sleeping boar husband.

It may seem cruel condemned a boar, but Mochan was still loved as a pet and well fed by Taanwibber, and though smelled foul and continually snored he slept at foot of her bed and kept her feet warm in winter.

When became within hearing range Taanwibber tauntingly enquired "Berrwynn the fearless, where is the child you promised, or have you come to offer more riches I do not need"?

His mission foreseen he unfortunately had nothing more to offer.

Whilst Taanwibber retreated to the cave for linen to dry her feet, Mochan awoke and whispered to Berrwynn. "There is something you can do to return me a human", and quoted a rhyme he thought cleverly composed "To kill a spell, you first kill the witch".

Though eligible administer of justice Berrwynn was reluctant to punish as Taaanwibber as yet had caused no injuries, and therefore he could not help Mochan without displeasing the gods.

When returned empty handed to the settlement Berrwynn was quizzed by tribal elders and mocked by young warriors as to inactive leadership.

Fortunately his wise councillor had returned and Berrwynn spent no time arranging a meeting, and spoke his problem. Androssan in deep thought silently sat stroking his long white beard and then stopped and broadly smiling declared, "Taanwibber and Meinir in coherence is an impossibility, fire and water never happily combine and soon will part in hate and extinguish each other, be patient;

and Mai the goddess of nature will solve your problem".

Meanwhile, Meinir had also adopted human form; and that of a most beautiful golden hair maiden, and she and fiery red haired Taanwibber became inseparable and basked in the sunshine of their new found companionships.

Excluding poor Mochan, they now shared Taanwibber's cave and all a boar most cared; food and comfortable warm bed was no more and he seethed with jealously.

Unobserved he often leeringly watched the two beautiful maiden/goddesses nakedly bathing in the tarn and afterwards grooming each other even more beautiful. He noticed after bathing habitually sat at the waterside combing and plaiting each other's waist long hair, and thereafter bent forward to admire their reflections mirrored in the water.

In his jealously enflamed porcine brain he slowly developed a brainwave, offering to comb and plaid their hair as to gradually gain their confidences.

However being a boar had its limits as he had hoofs instead of fingers and therefore difficult to plait hair, but in being split hoofs slightly benefited and he practised plaiting reeds from the lakeside until he had mastered the technique.

Thereon anxiously awaited his opportunity and when the goddesses as usual sat naked together on side the tarn on their toilet ritual Mochan approached and compliment them on their beauty. Then asked would it please them if he combed and then plaited their beautiful hair, and overwhelmed by his wily praise the vain goddesses giggled their approval.

The devious Mochan then set to work constantly combing and periodically dipping the comb in water to stretch the hair to longer strands whilst continuously amplified their already inflated egoism by complementing them on their alluring hair and voluptuous bodies.

The grooming went on every day until he was satisfied that they had come to implicitly trust him; and finally the day came whence he would commit his dastardly plan.

After hours of combing Mochan plaited the goddesses' hair, and instead of separately, gently platted together into one strong plait, the wily boar then tied a coloured ribbon at its end and secured to an already prepared round boulder.

Musing; "At last I have defeated divine spirits" and with a mighty heave of his strong porcine shoulders rolled the boulder into the deep water.

In its wake was dragged the gullible vain goddesses; and still in human form helplessly sank to bottom of the tarn.

In their exasperation they squirmed and fought to untie themselves from each other and the boulder and their struggles caused their opposite elements to furiously ferment emitting noxious gasses and killing all life within the tarn and its surroundings.

Sadly; and before the devious' porcupine Mochan's return to a warrior transpired

it was also unfortunately poisoned by the noxious gasses and tumbled from the bank into the fermenting waters.

The tarn has forever remained poisonous to all living creatures, and under thick yellow surface scum the evil goddesses are forever and safely entrapped.

Thereafter Berrwynn was credited with the tribe's deliverance, and knowing nothing of the circumstances of the goddesses' suppression he denied knowledge of the incident.

Androssan however advised him to say nothing and instead quietly accept their adoration.

****

The Two Vain Goddesses

Chapter XV

Ultimate

The Supreme Gods' proclamation. Berrwynn and Bronwen bid farewell to their son Maelor and ascend the mountains. Meet their friend Androssan the Ageless.

Androssan's final Revelation. ---- Hail the Gods. —Berrwynn Returns.

Taanwibber and Meinir firmly entrapped under the poisonous surface scum of the tarn Berrwynn assumed he was released of his vow and could now stay in Maengwyn.

He made his way happily, to meet Androssan and found him at their usual meeting place; and as on previous occasions he was in his usual state of celestial communication, and he had again to impatiently await his return.

When eventually opened his eyes; Berrwynn noticed on his facial expression that he was now going to make an important announcement, and pouring out two large goblets of wine Androssan handed one to Berrwynn sitting opposite.

Whilst slowly consumed the delicious liquid Berrwynn looked anxiously across wondering what they were celebrating,

Androssan then obliged his obviously questioning eyes; stating. "My dear Berrwynn, this is indeed your most glorious occasion, and what I am about to proclaim; its significance is far beyond what you have ever dreamt".

Pausing as to assert correct phrases, Androssan; and looking directly into Berrwynn's curious eyes, continued "Firstly, I am confirmed that you have successfully overcome hurdles orchestrated by the Supreme Gods. Thereon proclaim that they are extremely satisfied with your progress towards enhancement, and they have also a personal message for you".

Berrwynn was overawed that he; a mere mortal, was honoured by a message from the Supreme Gods, however its contents brought him no joy as sadly confirmed what he thought had overcome.

As he on behalf of the tribe's people had made Taanwibber a binding promise, it therefore could not be broken unless mutually agreed, and as to the goddess' present disposition; there was very little or no hope of annulment.

Berrwynn hoped Androssan would intervene on his behalf and change the situation, however as destined it was impossible, and the message also conveyed what painfully knew of Taanwibber's foredoom of a great pestilence if he ignored

When Berrwynn broke the sad news Bronwen she immediately assigned to accompany him, and furthermore swore eternal damnation on the fiendish Taanwibber, and also the evil river goddess Meinir.

Entombment in their watery prison; they were said to be heard laughing at Berrwynn's expatriation, but it was later confirmed were their screams from extreme burns of their adopted mortal bodies'; In Bronwen having deposited cartloads of quicklime in the tarn.

Accepting his inevitable destiny, Berrwynn learnt he had furthered progressed and was now through third stage of his inauguration, and one before his final elevation to the utmost prevalence of divine ascendancy.

A few days later he had again to meet Androssan, and whilst waited his arrival he gazed upwards at the mist shrouded waterfall and observed a superb rainbow arching over the high falling waters. Whilst admiring its clear multi colours, there suddenly came from a gap in above black clouds a single beam of light and which shone directly on him.

From amidst roar of falling water' Berrwynn heard a powerful voice proclaim.

"I am Idris the Supreme God of Cambria, and with confirmation of major gods, Gwydyr, Arran, Plymon, Vaan and Preseli, and goddesses Powyse, Deva, Mona, Hira and Dyfi, we have and unanimously agreed to your also deity".

"Berrwynn, you are soon to be proclaimed a god, and also Bronwen a goddess, go now and climb the twin peaks which overlook your lands, and there will be enthroned and thereon rewarded with the secrets of the universe"

"Future generations will revere you on your twin thrones of Cader Berrwynn and Cader Bronwen, and proclaimed the benevolent Gods of Maengwyn".

Though Berrwynn and Bronwen were to be honourably beatified, they however were much saddened to part from their beloved son Maelor and their tribe's people, but as preordained was inevitable they obey the Supreme Gods.

When came the day of departure, it seemed more a funeral cortège when Berrwynn and Bronwen's cart and engulfed in flowers was escorted by their son and mourning tribe's people along narrow lanes to the foot of the mountains.

When reached, Berrwynn and Bronwen alighted from the cart and sadly bid their people their final farewell, and last of all of their son Maelor; and now to be the leader of tribe.

Together; the two sad exiles began their ascent, and very soon they had disappeared from view into the swirling mountain mist, and rounding a rocky bluff they encountered a lone bearded figure. When neared they recognised it was their friend Androssan the Ageless; and as absent from their departure ceremony they had been concerned, and were now extremely pleased to see him.

Androssan proclaimed that he was tasked to escort the two to their honoured domain, and reaching their designated thrones, he further informed that he had one and the most fundamental secret to reveal.-

"I am known to you and tribe's people as Androssan the Ageless, and I now confirm I am also Idris, the Supreme God of Cambria.

Suddenly the sky was streaked with lightening flashes and deafening thundering and of which on impacting the earth caused the ground tremble, up-heave and opening great cavities.

In the darkness Berrwynn lost sight of Bronwen and bewilderingly staggered through the hellish turmoil aimlessly searching for her. Suddenly he felt a terrific force strike his head and destroying his helmet – which he had not realised wore.

Firstly numbed, but it now pained so extreme felt as if his head was splitting apart, and feeling his right lower arm warmed he found was pouring blood from a shoulder gash. However this was mostly dwarfed by the head pain and was only periodically aware by restrictive use of his right arm hanging limply at his side.

In excruciating pain and utterly exhausted aimlessly wandered through knee-high mud whilst avoided the best he could the rapidly water filling cavities.

Then he heard a familiar Liverpool accent profanely shout. "What the ******** hell are you doing? – Try'n be Aun' Sally for de' Huns or some-ting"?

Grabbed unceremoniously by the leg Berrwynn was dragged into a newly formed crater and only seconds before another thunderous explosion and his Scouse accented saviour was lifted by the blast and fell atop of him.

Laying at the side of the rapidly water filling crater Berrwynn noticed it reached knees and was so comfortingly cool longed it reached his painfully wounded shoulder and sooth away the pain.

When turned to his saviour lying half upon him he found was dead; and somehow recollecting an old friend called Joe Murphy he pulled his head around as to see his face. Berrwynn was shocked to discover was nonexistent, having been completely taken away by the hot flying metal and he would never know who saved his life.

The shock brought Berrwynn to his senses, and realising the danger of the cavity filling with water he tried to get out before was drowned. But under the weight of overlaying dead body and weak from his wounds, and however hard he tried he could not master the slippery climb to the crater ridge.

Lying there and in great pain listening to the continuous mysterious thundering noises intercepted with earth shaking flashes. Berrwynn wondered whether Supreme Gods had instead condemned him to this cold and wet underworld.

However, he had the one consolation Bronwen was not also there, and hopefully she was saved from this icy anti/inferno, and probably now warm in Nevol - though was possibly lonely.

After bout of depressive reflection he noticed the water in the crater was not increasing as he expected, and instead was draining into a dark culvert, and hoping to sooth his pains. He slid down the craters muddy side from under the dead body and into the culvert and lay in the cool soothing muddy water.

Suddenly he realised he was being carried by the current and though desperately struggled could do nothing to resist being taken downwards and forever increasingly colder. He had now no more energy to struggle and allowed the current to carry him what may, and eventually reaching a confluence of clearer water course he felt as if he was becoming warmer.

The warmth was increasingly invigorating his cold painful body, and seemed as if was now fastly arising higher and higher. Along the way he noticed lights flashing on and off; and similar to what had somewhere experienced a long time before.

Through barely opened eyes Berrwynn saw figures dressed in white standing near his feet and assumed they were the Supreme Gods, and hopefully changed their minds and awaiting his arrival. But when realised Bronwen was not also amongst them he was again devastated, and he wondered why she was not also in Nevol.

The white clad figures stood whispering and a matronly female; assumedly Averna came to him and put her soft cool hand on his throbbing forehead.

Bending over she then spoke, but Berrwynn could not understand what she was saying, and when he tried to speak his lips could not form the words his mind intended.

Berrwynn had then to close his eyes from the dazzling whiteness of his surroundings, and he knew no more.

Chapter XVI

<u>Awakening</u>

Field Hospital, near Ypres Belgium. Horrors of Passchendaele. Chaplain Idris Parry. Berrwynn meets nurse Annwen. Recovery and he returns home. Berrwynn and Annwen are married. Becomes a village school master. – The End.

Major Lalumiere the night duty surgeon passed slowly along the long line of beds in the field hospital ward, and as done many times before he picked up the clipboards attached to end of each bed and carefully scrutinised.

These patients were the latest batch from the Passchendaele front offensive of third battle of Ypres, and each day casualties arriving at the First Canadian Military Field Hospital near Popering in Belgium multiplied.

Though the hospital was more than ten miles from Ypres salient battlefront it was well within sounds of the thundering guns dedicated overworked medical staff had become oblivious to the discharges. Also enemy's continuous ground shaking exploding shells, but certainly not to the horrific human carnage it all caused.

The intensive enemy barrage not only caused immediate deaths but showering of exploding shells' casings; called shrapnel, also caused innumerable casualties and if not as often fatal otherwise suffered atrocious bodily wounds. He medical staff were persuaded as not to grimace at extend of these wounds as to minimise the patients awareness, however was difficult and especially for young and new staff.

Pierre Lalumiere was a graduate of the University School of Medicine Montreal, and when on his rounds he often compared to back home in Canada where mostly treated aged arthritics and young men involved in needless motoring accidents. Then had youthful hopes of a wonderful life in medicine but it all changed when the Germans invaded France, and now longed for the times when had time to leisurely chatted to his patients of latest baseball or ice hockey scores.

As many young men of his age Pierre volunteered for war service, enrolling in the Royal Canadian Medical Corps and sent to France of his ancestors, and since arrived was engaged in this very same field hospital just inside the Belgium border.

In wartime promotion is rapid, and in his extremely stressful and disturbing third year achieved promotion to Major Surgeon, however in brute reality of this war and which was hell on earth he had to somehow to disassociate. His remedy as to preserve his stability of mind from what he daily confronted indulged in much reading and writing poetry.

Nearing end of his rounds the Major hesitated at nineteenth and next to last bed in the ward, picking up the clipboard and reading he approached the unconscious patient whom had his head and right arm heavily bandaged. Pierre sighed and wondered whether his medical expertise could save his young life, and in native French language pointlessly muttered. "O my God, when will this mindless slaughter end"?

Putting the clipboard back on its hook he turned to his deputy and continuing in English said "See this young man here, I have a kid brother his age, thank God h'still in college, and if has any sense, stay there until the terrible carnage ends".

Seemingly for no apparent reason; or maybe to emphasize to his associate of his utter despair, Pierre Lalumiere the Major Surgeon once again picked up the clipboard, studied, and then proceeded to read aloud the patients medical record.

THE 2ND ROYAL CANADIAN MEDICAL FIELD HOSPITAL, POPERINGE

Patients No. & Name - *552339 Private John Berrwynn Evans*

Regiment& Battalion - *2nd Battalion, Royal Welch Fusiliers*

Patient's Age – *19.*

Casualty Date – *18 October 1917*

Date of Admittance – *18 October 1917*

Injuries – *(Shrapnel Impact) Suspected cranium fracture. Serious right shoulder wound,*

Condition – *Pulse weak, - Shows faint signs of regaining consciousness.*

Religion – *O.D. / Nonconformist.*

Relatives Informed – *In process*

Pierre's associate and deputy; Lieutenant Leonard J. Cooney was a graduate of the University of Ontario, thereafter subaltern at Toronto General Hospital, and he had also volunteered his services. But for a different reason; feared the war would end before called to enlist and miss his opportunity to travel to Europe, as on his salary it would take him many years to achieve this ambition.

Leon's troopship had landed in Liverpool seven months previous and was posted to a Military Hospital in Wiltshire where convalescing and disabled casualties of the war were firstly dispatched. His aspirations of seeing the Old World however was disappointingly curtailed as it was weeks before he had even the opportunity to visit London, and months before accomplished visiting his mother's birthplace.

It was indeed fortunate had taken this opportunity, as two weeks later he was shipped across the English Channel to Calais in France and immediately sent on to this present field hospital, and since his arrival he had had hardly a day's leave.

The latest batch of casualties held the Lieutenant attention more than usual as they were from a Welsh regiment, as possibly some could be from his mother's born village. However this made him to solemnly reflect; had not his mother previously emigrated he also may have been one of these poor casualties.

Whilst the Major read out the young patient's record, Lieutenant Cooney was looking at the wounded soldier's face and noticing his eyelashes flickering whispered his observation to his superior officer. Pierre was unconvinced; but returned to the patient's bedside, and then turning addressed the Lieutenant. "Your observation is correct", he declared "Young militaire has regained consciousness" and reducing his voice to a whisper he soberly added, "But seems of little avail as chances of his recovery is doubtful".

Accompanied white clad staff nurse approached the patient and held a glass of water to his lips, and of which he took a weak sip, she he put her hand on his forehead. To test his sensibilities she asked him his name, but his reply was so faint and imprecise they could not ascertain what he was saying, and the Major deliberated as whether he had also suffered brain damage.

Following the medical staff around the ward were military chaplains, and who after checking each bed's clipboard for the patient's religion, and if of appropriate sect spoke to them a few words of comfort.

The Reverend William Idris Parry had been chaplain for over two years and conducted more military funerals than cared remember, and though Church of England also served members of the nonconformist denominations.

Catching up with medical team Captain Parry was in time to hear the patient utter words and of which Major Lalumiere professed was gibberish, bending over the patient the chaplain spoke to him in a strange tongue. When received a hardly audible reply the chaplain straightened up, and smiling radiantly informed that the patient was mentally sound, as when asked his name replied it was Berrwynn.

The Major however was dubious of the chaplain's conjecture, and rechecking the clipboard expressed "According to his records his name is John", but ardent historian Idris Parry explained. "Where the patient comes from are generally called by a second name".

He then elaborated, "It was because of past Clergy's insistence on English forenames, and the mostly nonconformists indignantly responded by duplicating offspring's names, and invariably called by their native Welsh second name".

William Idris Parry came from border town of Oswestry where his father William Parry was employed in the Cambrian Railways' head offices as personal assistant to the director Mr Savin. Having achieved heights well beyond his working class dreams he furthermore eventually became a director, and the lucrative position afforded him a large middle class home on edge of town.

It also privileged his son Idris public school education in Shrewsbury and mixing with rich acquaintances such as Wilfred Owen of Plas Wilmot, and who also served on this very front; but as yet their paths had not crossed. Also David Davies; son of the entrepreneur coal mine and docks owner, and though in same regiment he was in another battalion serving in Palestine.

After Shrewsbury Idris had planned to go to Jesus College Oxford but as the war progressed he alike many others donned military uniforms, and a divinity student ensured him chaplain. At home Idris' parents spoke their native language, but he; and brought up amongst middle class Shropshire folk he however rarely conversed in his parents' tongue.

The wounded soldier, Private John Berrwynn Evans was the eldest son of a slate miner whom had become victim of slate lung; a prevalently disease caused by the breathing the deadly slate dust.

His father invalided; Berrwynn at fourteen became the family's breadwinner, and as only available work at his young age was farm labouring, subsequently he had to leave home to live on a farm. The farm consisted mostly of mountain grazing sheep, few cows, pigs and poultry, and was cultivated a little wheat and rye, but most fields were left to hay and harvested for the animal's winter fodder.

Berrwynn enjoyed the work and new freedom, but was uncomfortably miserable in cold and wet winter weather and with other farm hands he slept in the stable loft and warmed by heat rising from animals below. But the stench of the horses sweat and of their defecating was atrociously unbearable at first, and gradually he became accustomed.

On Saturday nights he returned home and proudly handed his mother the six shillings wages, usual rate was less, but the farmer; and relative, added an extra shilling to help ease the family's poverty.

Berrwynn stayed at the farm until when at sixteen years of age and eligible of a more enumerative employment in local slate mine, and partnered his father's old assistant doing piecework. The work was hard and dangerously done by light of candles in great caverns under the mountain, and relative to their wages it was sheer exploitation.

A workers union committee had been established trying to improve their outrageous working conditions and low wages, consequently relationships between miners and their employer sharply deteriorated. Leading to a long and bitter strike, but miners' stark impoverishment eventually forced them to concede to their employers' terms.

They returned to work at their previous pittance wage and awful conditions, and   triumphant mine employer refused re-admittance to whom they assumed were the instigators. As Berrwynn's father had previously been a force for many years in trying to form a trade union, they now excluded his young sixteen-year-old son.

Blacklisted; and slate mine the only industry, the family's income was now at a minimum and Berrwynn's younger sister and brother had also to leave school to assist the family and importantly retain their rented slate mine owned cottage.

Berrwynn considered emigrating to Alberta Canada with a farming assisted travel scheme, and whilst awaited reply to his application the war began and emigration was halted. Thereafter was sympathetically employed by the previous farmer at still very low wage of seven shillings and sixpence a week, but shortly afterwards the farm lands was requisite by the military; for war training.

His sister Mair employed at Pale; the local mansion, managed to acquire Berrwynn employment as assistant to the under gamekeeper, the Liverpool born Lucky Joe Murphy; and was so called as never admittedly backed a losing horse.

That was not all, he also cheekily supplemented his also meagre wage by inside poaching the owner; Colonel Crawford's prized game, naïvely young and under older man's influence Berrwynn also got involved. Selling their poaching gains; together with their permissible sale of snared rabbits and mole skins by arrangement with a travelling game dealer.

Berrwynn now began experiencing the thrills of growing masculinity enjoying the intimate favours of an upstairs maid five years his senior called Dervela, though purely physical as the maid had ambitions to escape from rural poverty.

Before long Dervela attracted the attention of her widowed employer Colonel Crawford nearly twenty years her senior, and becoming pregnant she was discreetly transferred to their London residence', and they were later married.

Berrwynn's sister Mair; and assessable to below stairs gossip, inferred the Colonel never questioned whether the babe was his own; and Mair was probably joking when also instigated that the baby was uniquely alike someone she knew.

Their poaching and secret sale of stolen game ended, when it was discovered by the head gamekeeper Mr Braithwaite, a typical bone headed ex-army sergeant and who viewed all life in black or white. Originally from Surrey he was unused to the habits and beliefs of rural native people whom regarded wild creatures' as common property, and traditionally assumed it was their right to take.

When summoned to appear before the magistrate; the wily Liverpool born under-keeper disappeared and joined the army, but it was sadly learnt that Lucky Joe's luck had this time deserted him, he was declared missing and presumed killed.

Colonel Crawford being also a magistrate could not officiate of his own case, and instead Berrwynn was summoned to appear before the slate mine owner, and who would happily consider sentencing him to long incarceration.

However, when it became known to Dervela she pleaded her husband to drop the charges, and reluctantly agreed if Berrwynn enlisted in the army, and needing to get away from the district he considered was fair.

Thereafter he enlisted in the Royal Welch Fusiliers, and after completing three months military training he was shipped to Calais and then on to Flanders.

Suspecting the patient had little time left in this world, and seeking his next of kin the chaplain picked up his pay-book laying with belongings besides the bed and opening he discovered that John Berrwynn Evans' parents lived near Bala. Knowing a nurse in a nearby ward came from near the town; the chaplain hurried over and informed her of the patient from her locality who was dying. But deaths' of innumerable young men was deeply disturbing to the young nurse and she was reluctant to add to the number by visiting patients in other wards. However; as he came from her neighbourhood she felt it was her duty to visit him and speak to him in own language to ease his passing.

The nurse; Annwen Roberts was also firstly employed in the Pale Mansion, and exceedingly assiduous was poached by an elderly spinster relative of the Colonel to care for her at their Regent's Park home in London. When the old lady died, Annwen and twenty three years old and unmarried had no wish to return home as wife of a poor miner, and fortunately attained a nursing post at Guy's Hospital.

During the Great War there circulated appeals for nurses to serve in France, Annwen and similar to local hero Betty Cadwaladr who nursed in Crimea, she also naïvely volunteered her services. However the wonderful foreign cities with their beautiful cathedrals she had expected to see never materialised and instead toiled day and night in horrific field hospitals' environment.

Nurse Roberts entered the ward, and sitting near the patient she laid her hand on back of Berrwynn's hand showing at end of his outstretched bandaged right arm and spoke to him in his native tongue. And feeling her feminine touch and hearing her Welsh voice Berrwynn slowly opened his eyes and looked up at her face, and he then opened his eyes wide and stared at her as in disbelief.

His eyes filling with tears he brought his other hand over and laid atop the nurse's hand, and choked with emotion he spoke only the one word, and assumedly said 'Annwen'; and concluded referred to the nurse; but no knew how knew her name.

The nurse lowered her head nearer his face as to hear him speak, and her pleasant young face very near his and enjoyed her close proximity and felt tempted to kiss her soft cheek. Abashed at his absolutely galling impulse! Berrwynn hurriedly averted his eyes and towards tall figure of the chaplain standing at end of his bed with his eyes tightly closed and assumedly praying.

He noticed the chaplains's clothes were a shade of green and concluded it was caused by daylight penetrating through the green tented fabric, and when raised his eyes he startlingly observed that his face was also green.

The revelation of the tall figure's greenish sober face struck a chord deep in Berrwynn's mind, and in trying to recollect its familiarity he momentary pictured him bearded and beggarly attired.

Whether it was the affect of morphine administered to ease his pain Berrwynn never knew; as an inner force within him in a clearer voice, called out *"Ple mae d' fardd* (Where's thy beard?) Hearing his question; the chaplain opened his eyes and momentary stared at the wounded soldier; and as if now recognised, he; and with a somewhat familiar rare smile answered in the ancient Celtic tongue,

"Ydi ddim eto, d'amser" (It's not yet, your time).

Whether Berrwynn imagined; however it soothed his mind and contentedly closed his eyes and entered into a peaceful sleep; dreaming of beautiful maiden goddesses dancing in wonderful flowered pastures.

When he awoke he felt happily refreshed, stronger and more alert of surroundings, and for the first time was now able to look around the ward and he now discovered the cause of a constant sound reminiscent of cascading water.

He now observed it was the wind flapping fabric doorway, and he later noticed that it was through this left side canvas door the deceased were taken to the mortuary. And also, the right hand door was for the incoming patients and those who were recuperated, but whether fortunate was not sure as many were horrifically mutilated and others blinded from enemy mustard gas.

Reverand Parry and Annwen's frequent welcomed visits greatly contributed to Berrwynn's psychological well being, Annwen's only Welsh book was of poems by Dewi Havesp and often recited to him until he was able to read on his own. Subsequently he also became to love the poet's countryside observations, and his witty semi religious compositions and his amusing ongoing poetical rage at the alcohol prohibitive Calvinistic Methodists.

Some months later Berrwynn was too greatly to miss' Annwen's companionship; as with only one day's notice he was moved to a medical unit near Calais port for repatriation to a convalescent hospital on Salisbury Plain in England. And after long and boring six months convalescence in Tidworth he was sent to Park Hall camp nearer his home for official accession of his disabilities.

Subsequently he was released from the army and returned home.

After initial excitement of his home coming Berrwynn began more and more to miss' Annwen's company, and looking back he concluded was mostly through her companionship he had maintained a will to recover. He was now convinced that he also loved her; and though they regularly corresponded, neither one had expressed love, as both remained uncertain of the others' true feelings.

The war resulted in immense shortage of school teachers and though unqualified Berrwynn was fortunate to acquire assistant teaching post at a local school, and at the time he constantly thought of how would earn a living when the war ended.

The headmistress encouraged him to apply for teacher training and he was indeed surprised when accepted, but penniless had thoughts of declining, and Dervela Crawford kindly helped pay his expenses.

When completed final examinations, Berrwynn alas became distraught at thought of failure and suffered recurrent horrific nightmares, reliving time in the trenches, and was in dire circumstances of the later known - post-traumatic stress.

Subsequently, he was interred in a psychological hospital dealing with casualties of shellshock and similar mental disorders and injuries, and fortunately after few months he gradually regained his health.

Due to the desperate need of nursing services, Annwen was not released until a nearly a year after the war had ended and she immediately visited Berrwynn in Cross House Hospital near Shrewsbury.

When again met were overwhelmed and scarcely hid their emotions, but whilst both realised were much in love neither one had the confidence as to express their true feelings, and both only shyly stressed how much they had missed each other.

Annwen was also in need of employment and only possible work was to return to nursing, and as to be near Berrwynn applied for a psychiatric nurse position at the same hospital. But a short time after she started the post Berrwynn had been allowed to return home.

As many experienced teachers were returning from war needing employment Berrwynn's numerous teaching applications brought only negative responses and he became depressed. He suspected it was due to stigma attached to mental illness and wondered whether ever be employed, and though loved and wished to marry Annwen would not burden with an unemployed mentally scarred husband.

However, being an experienced nurse she was best judge, and correctly suspected that Berrwynn had not proposed marriage because of his loss of self confidence due to his previous ill-health.

Having become a good friend of Berrwynn's sister Mair, Annwen let slip that she loved her brother and wished to marry him, and Mair whom was concerned for his health precautionary revealed to Berrwynn their conversation.

However, this was wonderful news to him, and confessed also wished to marry Annwen, but was still adamant would not marry until he was fully employed and able to provide for a wife and maybe children.

Mair found difficult to inform Annwen of Berrwynn's decision without revealing had betrayed her trust, however indicated he was also in love but lacked the confidence to propose marriage. Half jokingly, Mair informed it was now a leap year; and traditionally on the one extra day women may propose a marriage, and though Annwen probably heard the comment, did not reply.

Spring weather appeared early that year, and needing an outing after the long cold winter indoors Berrwynn borrowed his brother's motorcycle and with Annwen on the pillion they excitingly roared through the countryside. Feeling the nearness of her body and her arms tightly clutched around him aroused much of his long surpressed desires, and many years later Annwen confessed of similar experience.

Unintentionally they arrived at Pistyll Rhaeadr waterfall, but as early low sun shadowed searched until found a sheltered suntrap, and laying their old army overcoats on moss covered rocks they sat in the sunshine enjoying a picnic lunch.

Berrwynn lovingly gazed at Annwen sitting opposite, and noticing the sunlight reflecting off the sparkling waters dancing on her face he searched his mind for a long ago familiarity. Finally he remembered was from a childhood school book of an intriguing sketched portrait of the Celtic moon goddess, Cerridwen.

After drinking a bottle of Guinness that Annwen had bought him and comfortably relaxed unintentionally fell asleep and when awoke he found her sitting on a rock with her bare feet dangling in the icy cold water. Unlike himself she seemed nervously uncomfortable and eventually; and as if plucked up courage she stated; had something very important to ask him.

Avoiding looking into his eyes and profusely blushing; Annwen blurted out. "I dearly love you Berrwynn, and I know you love me, and I wish we marry".

Highly embarrassed; she burst into tears, and reaching over Berrwynn held her hard worked hands and retorted "My dearest Annwen, I dearly love you also, but I will only marry when I am fully employed and never a burden to you".

He now anxiously awaited Annwen's reply, and he was much relieved when asserted that she understood his concern, and now knowing that were to marry as soon he was financially able to support satisfied her, and ever gently they kissed.

Having experienced nearness of each other's bodies when clasped her arms about him on the motorbike their physical passions were somewhat aroused and were anxious to enjoy what they should have been experiencing in their younger age.

Relaying their old army overcoats in between the moss' covered boulders they passionately clutched each other and abandoning all restrain; they and within the roaring of descending waters striking the rocks below, consummated their love.

The Crawford's now lived near Shrewsbury and influential in county affairs, Mair and concerned of her brother contacted Dervela requesting her aid in securing Berrwynn a teaching post or similar.

Following her request Berrwynn was offered an interview with the more enlightened officers of the Shropshire Education Authority, and was exceptionally thrilled to achieve a teaching position at a village junior school.

Their fortunes now at last having moved into a favourable aspect they decided to immediately marry whilst the gods still smiled on them.

Turning up at the door of the quiet Guilsfield village's vicarage to meet the vicar was more than little daunting, and a testimony to Berrwynn's recovery in that he was able to joke – "It's worse than going over the top".

Lifting the heavy brass knocker Berrwynn let it drop and loud respond broke the intense silence, and a while later a maid neatly dressed in starched white apron answered the door. When explained their mission the maid replied, "Momentary the Reverend is busy writing his sermon, if you follow me to the library I will inform him, and I trust he will see you as soon as he is able".

Looking at the books lining the shelves Berrwynn noticed that besides the usual theological books there were a few non religious and also controversial titles and it eased his anxiety that he had not to meet a sanctimonious high church cleric.

They did not have to wait long until the library's solid wooden panelled door was opened and a tall figure bowed his head to pass under the lintel, and straightening up he stood a little past the threshold and quietly scrutinised the visitors.

Stunningly, they all instantly recognised each other, and who was most surprised was impossible to tell, and they warmly shook hands with Reverend Idris Parry, and the following hours they happily spent reminiscently conversing.

Idris related that when released from army service he had turned his back on furthering his education and realised a dream which kept him sane when was conducting the thousands of military funerals. That of returning home and be nothing more than priest in a quiet rural parish, and where he could spend his time contentedly reading and writing.

As if afterthought, the young couple declared they had originally come to the vicarage as wished to be married, and Idris Parry was delighted fate or maybe God had guided them to his church, and he instantly granted their joyous union.

The marriage of Berrwynn to Annwen was officiated by Idris Parry in the little parish church; and having very little money and instead of a honeymoon moved house to where he was soon to be engaged in his teaching career.

They had now achieved utmost fulfilment, Berrwynn recovered his health, and fully employed as a schoolmaster, Annwen was happily married to a loving husband, and she later became mother of four healthy children.

Looking north-west from their hillside cottage home near Nesscliffe village on the outskirts of Shrewsbury distant peaks of the Berrwyn Range of mountains was a familiar sight.

For most of the year these two major peaks are only hazily distinguishable from lesser nearer peaks, but in winter when cloaked in snow are very prominent and

from afar are perceived as two pallid faced Gods.

The End

Cader Berwyn and Cader B'onwen peaks

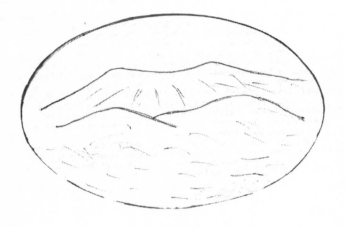

Lightning Source UK Ltd.
Milton Keynes UK
26 February 2010
150651UK00001B/5/P